M

The Wife's Redemption

BERYL WHITE

ROMANCE
PUBLISHING

COPYRIGHT

Title: The Wife's Redemption

First published in 2021

ISBN: 9798772608128 (Print)

CONTENTS

1

THE PURCHASE OF A LIFETIME

"Five guineas, and the girl is mine, you say?" enquired the young man.

"Yes. Exactly. It seems a fair price to secure the offer."

"I agree, Sister, very reasonable."

Reclining back in the plush leather chair, opposite the craggy-faced mother superior of Whitechapel's "Deserving Woman's Christian Mission," thirty-year-old Thomas Beadle swallowed hard.

Fidgeting, he picked at some non-existent specks of dust on his brown corduroy trousers. *'Anything to avoid eye contact,'* he mused. *'I don't want her gazing into my soul and finding something she shouldn't.'*

The pious woman reviewed the paperwork on her desk.

"And what are your plans now? If I might ask, Mr Beadle?"

'The truth won't go down well.' With deepening concern, he sucked in a silent lungful of air through his tightly

pursed lips, desperate for the delay to give his brain time to think of a suitable response. *'Got it.'*

> "The plan is a life of domestic service at my house in Abingdon. The apprenticeship will be worthwhile for the right candidate, I assure you. I am so convinced of the merits of this venture, Sister, I am completely happy to waive the apprenticeship fee owed to me by the mission."

He had planned this moment meticulously, ever since he was an undergraduate in philosophy at Corpus Christi, Oxford, and he didn't want to make a silly mistake at this late stage. Not when he was this close to securing a girl that would meet his needs. In that critical moment, anything to sweeten the deal for the orphanage would have been acceptable to him.

Sister Nancy looked over the top of her glasses, inspecting every inch of the applicant before her, who seemed, on the surface, to be an educated, respectable, if somewhat dishevelled, man. *'His tie is a little crooked and his hair a little unkempt. Those black shoes lack shine.'*

His gut clenched as he picked up on her concerns.

> "I assure you there will be thorough training provided throughout their placement with me. I'm grateful for the opportunity to nurture these orphans. I am sure they will appreciate the training far more than a novice I might recruit from an agency."

"I have to say your generous gesture to take them on at your own expense will make a significant improvement to the living standards of the girls and women still living here at the Christian mission. The costs of running the mission are not insignificant. Every bit of extra funding helps. Ten guineas will certainly help us."

"May I ask your name please, young man? Reverend Bennett did tell me earlier, but I forgot. The joys of getting older, you see."

"Wentworth," replied Thomas, "Sir Richard Wentworth. Here's the letter of intent you asked for in your last letter."

He handed over a note penned on a stolen piece of Sir Richard's official headed paper from the House of Lords, complete with a forged signature, then discreetly wiped the damp palms of his hands on his trousers. Sister Nancy scanned the note. Her body language suggested she felt everything was in order, which was a welcome sight for Thomas.

"I must say, it's an excellent opportunity for our orphans to take up employment with a respected politician like yourself. Quite often, they end up with an industrialist or at a craftsman's household. But one of the establishment? Well, that's quite a leap for our girls."

Thomas smiled politely even though the compliment was directed at somebody else.

"They will be ready for collection tomorrow. We'll get them inspected for lice and cleaned up and presentable," explained sister Nancy.

"They?" queried Thomas. "When I spoke to Reverend Bennett, I thought the arrangement was for me to apprentice a single girl."

"Ah, yes, about that. Recently, the board of governors changed our policy. Things are a little different to when since you first contacted us, Sir—"

Sister Nancy scanned the paperwork again with impatience.

"—Sir Wentworth. Now we insist that two girls enter service together. It's less upheaval for them. It provides some continuity in their young lives, if you will. And the Lord himself knows they have experienced enough hardship and upheaval. I am sure you appreciate why a smooth transition into service is critical for them."

Thomas nodded absent-mindedly as he reformulated his secret plan once again. All his previous attempts to snare a woman for himself had failed, and he didn't want another failure adding to the long list. Not now, at the eleventh hour. Not when he was so close to finally getting his unorthodox strategy implemented. He forced a smile he hoped looked benevolent.

"We find that the girls settle better and are thus more useful to their new masters if they both start their new lives at the same time."

This was not what Thomas was expecting at all. The finer details of his plan were now in jeopardy. Known for having a loose tongue and a habit of speaking his mind, he hoped evidence of his deception would not slip out under duress.

"That makes perfect sense," he said, puffing out his chest to feign confidence and acceptance. "It is important to me that my home life is simple and peaceful too. The last thing I want is tears and tantrums in my household."

There was a knock at the door.

"Come in," growled Sister Nancy.

Another young man poked his head around the corner of the doorframe.

"I'm so sorry I'm late. The traffic across London Bridge was just awful."

"I am Daniel Astley, Sister, a close associate of this fine fellow," he said as he slapped Thomas on the back, pulling up a chair before he was invited to sit.

A stern-faced Sister Nancy looked on, irritated by Astley's uncouth demeanour.

"You're just in time, Daniel. It's time for me to make my choice."

Astley fought to hide a wide grin. They had talked of nothing else but Thomas's plan ever since Beadle confessed to dreaming it up back in halls at Oxford.

"Choices, not choice," corrected Sister Nancy.

Daniel looked puzzled. The nun stood up and collected her papers, then strode for the door, her habit billowing behind her.

"Don't worry, I'll explain later," whispered Thomas.

"I'll leave you two gentlemen to talk. Excuse me for a moment. I'll check if the girls are ready for inspection."

"Thank you, Sister," said Thomas, bolt upright in his chair, looking like the new boy at a boarding school trying to impress the headmaster.

"I presume you will make your own choices rather than act upon our recommendation?"

"Yes, I think it's best that we choose, Sister. The sooner we build some rapport with the apprentices, the sooner they will listen, learn and perform their duties to our satisfaction."

"As you wish, Sir Wentworth."

Her voice trailed off as she paced down the corridor.

"What's this about girls?" said Daniel, the confirmed bachelor, with a glint in his eye. "I hope there are some fine fillies here at the mission."

Thomas rolled his eyes.

"That is not the point of my experiment, Daniel, as you well know. The whole process is governed by precise philosophical rules set down in the text we read at Corpus Christi. How many more times do I have to explain?"

"Quite a few," said Daniel, grinning with playful enthusiasm.

Much as he liked Thomas, he was a strange, insular fellow with some very eccentric characteristics, all driven by his head's ideological leanings more than by his heart. Very much a social pariah, when challenged, Daniel would joke Thomas was 'excellent to have around for entertainment value if nothing else.'

He turned to his friend.

"I am confused, Thomas. You only need one girl for your project."

"It's new rules I'm afraid we need. We have to take two because they settle better at their new residence."

"I see," said Daniel eagerly. "So, we'll have one each, perhaps?"

"It depends if they pass muster," tutted Thomas. "I might end up with no suitable girls and have to start again. It all depends on how they perform. Although goodness knows what will happen if the mission finds out I am not Richard Wentworth. If anyone discovers we're unmarried, they won't let the girls stay at our homes, and all these Christian orphanages are in close communication with each other."

"Quite," said Daniel with a beam, thrilled at being part of the deception, hoping that he would get to keep a girl.

Although handsome, he, too, had been unlucky in love. Suitable girls were put off because of his association with his roguish friend. To Daniel, Thomas's whole plan seemed like a fairy tale—plucking a pretty girl from poverty and giving her a better life, moulding her to perfection. He hoped his experience with the scheme might have a similar beneficial ending, especially now there were two girls. *'One each.'* he mused.

Falling into a trance, he daydreamed of eloping with his princess and living happily ever after in some far-flung corner of the empire. Lost in his reverie, Daniel slumped like a rag doll in his chair, goggle-eyes staring at the ceiling.

The door creaked open, and Sister Nancy reappeared. Although Thomas usually delighted in flouting society's rules and norms, he glared at his friend just for once, nodding for him to sit up straight. *'Doesn't he understand more understand more decorum is required whilst the ink dries on the deal?'*

"You can come through now, gentlemen. The girls are the sewing room."

The two men strolled down a faded corridor, the once white walls looking drab and dingy, even against the nun's billowing jet black habit.

"Your money will pay for a much-needed lick of paint here," Nancy advised.

The sewing room was vast with row after row of machines. An adolescent girl sat at each wooden workbench, stitching the hems on cotton blankets. Much younger children, barely older than infants, darted in between the tables, gathering up finished work, collecting up scraps of cloth, or discarded empty cotton reels.

"It is a way that the orphans can earn their keep at the mission," said Sister Nancy as she led the men down the main aisle. "The blankets will be used for the older single or battered women who seek shelter here at the mission. It's so much safer than a lodging house full of drunks and reprobates. And there is less sinful temptation here, of course. We ensure the women lead good Christian lives when they are under our care. Liquor, tobacco and personal male visitors are not allowed under any circumstances."

Daniel decided the lodging house sounded a lot more fun, and he would make a beeline for there if he ever fell on hard times before turning his mind back to the matter in hand.

His eyes scanned the room, looking for the prettiest girl with the softest, most feminine curves. Thomas, on the other hand, looked for the most productive girl and had little interest in any of their faces or figures.

A beautiful specimen caught Daniel's eager eye. That was it. His mind was made up. As the girl concentrated on keeping her seams as her leg pedalled furiously, the young man stared at her. The nape of her neck was smooth and as pale as ivory. Her hair was pinned up neatly in a bun, and he imagined her loosening it as it tumbled around a gossamer-thin nightdress. Then, with glee, he turned to signal to Thomas he had found 'his one,' even though he would not be responsible for her in any way.

Thomas had a different set of criteria entirely. He chose a strong-looking girl towards the back of the room. She was carrying a heavy bolt of fabric as if it were nothing. Like a man from the Highlands with a caber, she staggered as she walked over to the cutting table and then let the roll tumble onto it with a thud.

> "How many more times! Be careful, Lucretia. If that slides off, you'll knock one of the little one's senseless." Sister Nancy reprimanded as Daniel looked over to see Thomas was besotted with the clumsy but eager creature.

'That will be his choice, no doubt.' Daniel chuckled to himself, laughing harder still when Thomas nodded in Lucretia's direction to indicate his preference.

Sister Nancy paced around the room inspecting the girls' work as Daniel glanced at the fair-skinned maiden he had noticed. Thomas saw none of the prettiness, his eye taken by the precise rhythm of her pedalling and the accuracy of her stitching. Luckily for Amelia, the two men's requirements overlapped since Thomas would have the final say. It was his cunning scheme, after all.

"So, gentlemen, have you selected the two candidates?" asked the nun.

The men nodded.

"Good. Please come with me."

The trio went over to the corner of the room to talk privately. Sister Nancy was keen not to upset those girls who were overlooked on this occasion. Whilst she and Reverend Bennett did their utmost to make life comfortable for the orphans, everyone knew they would have considerably more freedoms and enjoyment in life if they were to have a benevolent master with a country pile. Sir Richard Wentworth was as well known for his charity work and philanthropic donations as he was for his impressive Georgian home. Sister Nancy had a good feeling in her bones about her latest placement.

As each man indicated his preference with a subtle glance, Sister Nancy gave a wry smile as she made a mental note.

"So, Amelia and Lucretia. As you wish. Until tomorrow, noon, Sir Wentworth. I will get the girls ready for collection right away."

"Thank you, Sister."

As they made their way out, Thomas fumbled in his blazer pocket and pulled out his wallet.

"I know I have waived the usual five guinea fee you pay me for board and lodgings for the girls, but please take this extra payment. I am sure you will spend the money wisely on those who remain here."

He handed over a crisp ten-pound note.

"Thank you very much, Sir Wentworth," trilled the sister. "The girls will have some extra rations of bread with their soup now. You have been most kind."

She escorted the two wealthy guests to the main reception area.

"Until tomorrow then."

"Yes, sister. Thank you. I promise you I will take the greatest care with my new wards."

The two men skipped down the short steps from the mission to the pavement. Outside, Thomas's long-suffering valet, Victor, was waiting for both of them, perched up high on the coach's driver's bench. It had been a long afternoon, killing time in the wintery drizzle.

He observed them trying to glean whether or not their mission to the mission had been a success. As the two men hunched into the wind, it was hard to tell.

"How did it go, Mr Thomas, Sir?"

"Very well, very well indeed, Victor, although there is a slight issue."

Victor raised his eyebrows as he peered down at his master's face.

"They want us to take two girls, "added Astley.
"One each, perhaps?"

Victor looked worried. He jumped down from the driver's platform and opened the Brougham carriage door.

"For goodness' sake, stop fussing, Victor. I'm not an invalid!" snapped Thomas. "I can open the door for myself, you know."

"Yes, I know, Sir."

"And don't call me 'Sir'."

"Yes, Mr Thomas," said Victor, reprimanded once again for failing to meet his master's exacting standards.

It was a fine line to tread. Onlookers expected certain aspects of etiquette to be observed, the same things that free-spirited Thomas railed against. No matter what he did, someone would give him an ear-bashing.

Victor waited for Thomas to close the door himself then hopped into the driver's seat. Then, gently, he whipped the reins on the back of his horse, and the burgundy and gold carriage made its way across London towards their cosy Sussex Gardens hotel for the evening.

Back inside the mission, a bell rang out, signalling that the day's work was finished. The girls had to contain their eagerness to run away from their sewing machines, else Sister Nancy would give them a telling off. Bored to tears with the monotony of the work, two 15-year-old girls began to fight to be the first to navigate the door that led back to the orphan's dormitory.

The bickering was quite toxic at times as tempers frayed more their threadbare uniform cuffs.

Sister Nancy intervened.

"Lucretia! Amelia! That is enough!

'I shall be so pleased to finally be free of their wayward behaviour,' thought the nun. 'Tomorrow can't come too soon.'

Amelia had ended up at the mission on the night of her birth, left on the doorstep by her mother. No one had pieced together it was a local girl who, alone and terrified, had given birth behind Prospect Street's Little Drummer Boy pub. In the morning, the girl told her parents the baby was stillborn. It was an easy lie to perpetuate. Lacking enough money for proper meals, her tiny baby bump was easy to hide in winter under a shawl. None of the neighbours knew the girl was in the family way.

Officials didn't concern themselves with the matter either. As more and more of the underclass crammed themselves into the tenements, the authorities shrank away from investigating the horrors going on there. The police only ventured along the road if a murder case compelled them to visit. No one knew or cared about the latest infant to emerge. For the girl's family, it was a loose end that had been dealt with.

In the dead of night, the girl, still a child herself, washed and cleaned the infant with a bucket of water she had hidden a few days earlier near the empty beer barrels stored out in the yard.

Under cover of darkness, she hid the baby in a carpetbag, praying the thing wouldn't scream as she struggled to the back door of the mission. The young mother looked around furtively, hoping she had not been spotted, then left the child, still in the bag, with a scruffy note scribbled on a scrap piece of paper stuffed inside. It explained that the mother could not look after the child since it had been born out of wedlock, and the father had absconded on hearing the news rather than staying to do the right thing.

The young girl kissed her hand then rested it on the baby's head. Her cold, bloodied knuckles rapped on the service door to the mission, then she slipped into one of Whitechapel's inky-black alleyways and into anonymity.

Sister Nancy had opened the door, almost tripping over the wriggling bundle as she looked out to see who had knocked. On seeing the note, she knew finding the mother would be impossible. The mother didn't want to be found and would be hidden in a distant rookery in minutes. Looking for the lass would be doomed to failure. Thus, poor little Amelia had never known what it was like to have parents institutionalised from her very first day of life.

Lucretia had had a different start to life. Her doting parents brought her up until she was twelve and had only spent the last three years in the orphanage. As the only child that had survived, Lucretia was the apple of her parents' eyes. She was very much loved and knew what it was like to be pampered, even if her mother and father were almost destitute. They may have been poor, but they were very loving. The hole left when her parents suddenly died of consumption within weeks of each other was never going to go.

This more salubrious upbringing had given Lucretia a sense of entitlement and a feeling that people should naturally want to do things for her, rather than relying on her own initiative like Amelia.

These opposing outlooks became a bone of contention between the girls.

Amelia was much more independent and got on with what she was told to do, rather than questioning or expecting someone else to pick up the slack, like Lucretia.

No matter how badly behaved the orphans were, the staff at the mission were still keen philanthropists and did what they could to educate and support the orphans and impoverished young women that called upon their help.

Money was tight, but they did what they could to nourish and nurture. Reverend Bennett knew there were plenty of wealthy childless couples who would adopt a child or else give them a good start in life, with a thorough grounding in the skills required to be a competent domestic servant.

For the couples, the children from the mission were a joy to take on. Compared to orphans from the workhouse or reforming schools, they were disciplined thanks to the rigid timetable they followed. They were also well-educated, thanks to the donations of books given to the orphanage library and a string of undergraduate tutors from the University of Cambridge, who were linked with Tynedale Hall. As well as practising their skills in the fields, they were also keen to share their learning and more basic education with the orphans

As orphans, they knew they would have to be independent, and thus, were more compelled to learn than other children at ragged schools that still had the theoretical cushion provided by their parents to insulate them from the hardships of adult life.

At dinner, Sister Nancy placed Amelia and Lucretia at opposite ends of the dining hall. When they were kept apart, the squabbling soon ended, and they were well behaved once more. Sister Nancy hoped that there was enough room at Thomas Beadle's house to separate them, else they would fight like cat and dog.

She took Wentworth's note from her pocket explaining that he was happy to take on a child and educate it in the ways of domestic service. She didn't know that Thomas Beadle and Daniel Astley had forged the note to hide the fact that as single men, they would never have been allowed to take on two girls unchaperoned.

2

THE ANXIOUS WAIT

Thomas Beadle hurtled through the rotating doors of the hotel, keen on avoiding any social interaction. Several eyes in reception turned to see who the madman was. He bolted for the stairs and leapt up them two at a time. Daniel was in his wake, sweating profusely but desperate to keep up with his friend. Even further behind was Victor, who had had to battle to park the carriage and bring in a small wooden trunk stuffed with textbooks rather than clothes.

The armchairs by the bay window were two heavy Chesterfields. Thomas flopped into the left one and immediately loosened his tie.

"Drink?" Daniel asked.

"Definitely!"

A breathless Victor arrived, carefully negotiating the doorway with the trunk, eyeing his master for where to put it.

"Excellent. Bring that here, will you?"

Victor practically dropped the trunk to the floor, unable to carry the weight of it any longer. Thomas flung the lid open and rummaged around for his 'bible', but not a Christian bible, his bible, a specific philosophical text. It was a book that had made a deep impact upon him in his undergraduate days at Oxford. Within days there was to be another big change in his life.

Thomas's father had died when he was young, and his inheritance had lain untouched in a trust fund ever since. His mother was given a small stipend to fund the household for her and her son, but now, Thomas is on the cusp of a significant sum of money.

It wasn't the money per se that was important to him. It was the freedom that the money could buy if he ever needed it. He had prided himself on his simple and frugal lifestyle. He wasn't into formality, frippery, and finery — —but he was into freedom and free will.

He decided the money was merely a financial cushion to insulate him from having to comply with society's whims—something that he usually avoided at all costs.

He pulled a book out of the trunk. His fingers traced along the gold lettering adorning the cover: 'Forging a fruitful marriage. An experiment in social engineering,' by Edouard Giseau. It was the book that had been the catalyst to his plan for one girl—and now, two. A crystal glass hovered in his field of view.

"Thanks, Daniel," he said, before taking a large slurp of whiskey and giving a satisfying sigh. He loved the feeling of the burn and the sting of the liquor in his nose, as he thought it sharpened his senses rather than dull them. Single malts were one of his few extravagances.

He opened the book at the first chapter, careful not to crease the spine, and he began musing to himself.

"Rather than rely on Cupid and the season to find a wife, Daniel, I shall rely on the principles of philosophy, a far safer option, wouldn't you say?"

Both graduates from Oxford University, they had good debating skills and inquiring minds. Daniel had turned his to being a fully-fledged lawyer and was practising at Lincoln's Inn. But knowing the inheritance was coming, Thomas had abandoned his studies, just before qualifying, much to his proud mother's chagrin. He told himself he could always pick it up later if he ever hit hard times.

"This idea of yours, Thomas, it's crazy," warned Daniel. "I appreciate the rigour that went into writing the book. Giseau clearly understood a lot about morals and ethics, brotherhood, and family, but I get the feeling he didn't really understand people— women in particular."

"Fiddlesticks," said Thomas. "It's very much like the arranged marriages they have in India, wouldn't you say? Where people are matched based on their potential? What they can bring to the family and the partnership? Rather than purely because they get a stirring in their loins. A deciding factor that ranks tremendously on your decision making, Daniel?"

Daniel chuckled. As well as being opinionated, he thought Thomas would never get a wife of his peculiar habits. His shunning of societal norms meant he liked to wash in a stream rather than at a basin. Beadle delighted in his non-conforming attitude. He was creative, intense, curious, some might say, idealistic in his outlook, and took delight in the concept of a simpler life.

He was obsessed with developing himself. All his hobbies related to activities where progress could be measured, such as archery and hitting the bull's eye, or landing a large fish, all signs of skillfulness and mastery.

In his childhood, his mother had known he was different from other boys in the area. He was highly intelligent, which made him appear bossy and aloof, but really, he was just a determined young chap keen to forge his own way in the world.

Victor, his live-in valet and his dowager aunt, Susan, despaired their master's unusual living, particularly his eating habits. After slaving over the range, Susan would grind her teeth when he would mix a starter, a main course, and a dessert onto one plate, 'because it streamlined the eating process'.

Victor thought it made a strange and unpalatable concoction and couldn't understand why anyone would entertain such a practice. Heaven forbid he tried it in front of a lady at a restaurant! Victor thought she would run a mile.

"Thomas! Thomas!" hissed Daniel, but he didn't get a response.

So often, Thomas was in his own little world and lost interest in the opinions or company of others around him.

"Thomas!" Daniel barked again.

"Oh right, yes. Sorry."

Ashamed, Thomas picked up the book defensively and hid his face behind it, so only his eyes were visible above the cover.

"I've done it again, haven't I?"

"Yes," chuckled Daniel. "It's a good job you are an only child, Thomas. You would have driven your siblings mad with this eccentric behaviour of yours. I've only known you for a few years, and it grates on me tremendously at times. Now, don't argue, but I'm going to pour you another extra-large measure of firewater in the hope that you relax."

"But how can I relax, Daniel? Tomorrow, the plan begins in earnest. The experiment. The challenge. My future. It all starts tomorrow with the arrival of—"

Thomas suddenly looked blank.

"Amelia and Lucretia?"

"Yes, them."

"You'd better learn their names by tomorrow, else they'll be disappointed. They are not new hens for the yard, Thomas. They are people. With—names!"

"Yes. Amelia and Lucretia. Amelia and Lucretia," Beadle reminded himself under his breath.

Thomas's thinking had got even more unpredictable and erratic since Daniel, Richard Wentworth, and a few other Oxford alumni introduced Thomas to the local Royal Science and Art Society.

Although the society was full of people with curious minds keen to expand their understanding of the world around them, they all thought Thomas was in a different league altogether.

As a confirmed bachelor, they wondered how his life might pan out. Given his strong rebellious streak, once he'd read enough evidence to make up his mind, no amount of contrary opinion would change it.

"My plan is simple, Daniel, as I keep telling you. I want a plain and simple wife. A human being that could be considered more of a 'functional unit' rather than a lover. More like a dowdy, heavy-duty mangle, an excellent performer, but not in a glitzy music hall sense. Who would want a preening, peacocking society wife, expecting gifts, flowers, and holidays on the French Riviera? My wife will have everything she needs at home. She too will crave a simple life."

"Like the mountain girl?" added Daniel with a sigh.

"Precisely! Once it gets out to this season's debutantes that my inheritance is due before the year is out, I dare say the vultures will start circling, looking to get their claws into. No doubt they will try to tear pounds of inheritance from me, like pounds of flesh from a carcass."

"Don't be so melodramatic, Thomas, for goodness' sake."

"I've been pondering this for many years, Daniel. What I need to do—"

"—erm—have done," Daniel corrected.

"—is procure the raw materials from which to fashion a wife that will suit my requirements. Now, I have secured the candidate."

"Candidates—"

Thomas sighed, tiring of being rebuked.

"I need to plan for the living arrangements. We will not have a normal, what you might call 'romantic' arrangement, of course. It will be purely practical. In a few years, when we are married, we will have separate beds to get a good night's sleep. Surely that's a good thing? A tired mind is an unthinking mind, whereas a fresh mind can discover all that the world has to offer."

"Yes, Thomas. A stroke of genius, that," said Daniel, humouring him. "These girls, I wonder how long it will take to educate them? I presume they're able to read and write in a basic fashion?"

"I'm not expecting 'Abelard's dialectic' in terms of discussion and rigorous debate, Daniel. But reading should be a given, I suppose? I would imagine the Sunday school teachers will have worked hard to improve the girls' literacy."

"Yes! It helps them read the bible. After all, what young mind doesn't enjoy religious study?" groaned Daniel.

"Anyone who follows Mr Darwin, I expect?"

"Erasmus or Charles?"

"Both!" said Thomas with a grin.

"I wonder how long they've been institutionalised? That will have a bearing on their life experiences, passions, pursuits, and interests, I suppose. "

"Passions? I thought this wasn't a romantic arrangement?" Daniel teased.

"Tut tut, Daniel. This is serious. I think a girl who's been with the orphanage for most of her life will be easier to mould, wouldn't you say? More disciplined? Not tainted by the trappings of modern life.?"

"Possibly, Thomas, possibly," replied Daniel, preferring not to tell his friend about how many a lone, penniless girl topped up their income in the dark Whitechapel alleys.

Thomas's understanding of women was not helped by him being something of a mummy's boy. His mother had educated him at home after the sudden death of his father when young Tom was just six. That early feminine influence had forged Thomas's curious take on life.

Traditional male careers and pursuits held no interest. Mrs Beadle's endeavours to educate the boy had worked well to start with, and he earned a scholarship at a prestigious boarding school. Unfortunately, he developed smallpox in his first term and fell behind in his studies. Sadly, as he recuperated, he failed to get the grades needed to stay at his mother's chosen school, and he ended up at a lesser establishment. One silver lining was that it was closer to Oxford and easier for her to visit him, and their bond remained strong.

His mother's idea was to train as a lawyer, based on a chat with Daniel over a picnic one day. However, Thomas never warmed to the idea. 'Far too conventional', he felt.

"Will you ever finish your law training, Thomas?" Daniel asked as he swirled the last of his golden malt in his tumbler.

"Only if my inheritance runs out, I expect," Thomas joked. "However, I shall eat porridge three times a day to save money and make sure that I never ever have to take up such a hideous career."

He put down the book, giving up on reading until bedtime when he wouldn't be interrupted every five minutes by his extrovert friend.

"I'll confess, Daniel. Elements of the legal profession are 'palatable'. I like the mental challenge of coming up with a defence or a prosecution case. I like debating in my head, anticipating the opposing counsel's argument. I'm not so fond of performing in front of an audience. The courtroom is a big theatre, is it not? The barrister must pay attention to intonation, pace, and body language to persuade, much like orators such as Aristotle, Socrates, or Plato might debate in one of Pericles's courts in Ancient Greece. "

"If you say so, Thomas."

"As I told the Science and Art Society, my wife will enjoy literature and science, as well as moral and patriotic philosophy."

"But remember when you tried to help Wentworth with his wayward son? That didn't end well, did it?"

Sir Richard Wentworth had taken an interest in Thomas's project and had offered him the opportunity to train his boy in some of Giseau's methods, particularly building a stoic character and an inquiring mind in the youth. However, the experiment failed. Thomas's strict teachings and austere recommendations caused the young boy to rebel, and the project was abandoned. Wentworth decided an overbearing headmaster at Eton would be more effective in taming the lad and turning him into a proper gentleman.

Thomas's one-track mind returned to the textbook.

> "Here's another important part," he said, jabbing at the text. "My wife will be as simple as a mountain girl in her dress, diet and demeanour. Yet, she will be as fearless and intrepid as a Spartan wife or any Roman heroine. You see, it is not my fault that such a creature cannot be found. It is not my fault that I have exacting standards. But being unable to 'find' one does not mean I cannot 'make' one. This type of philosophical romance, this perfect partnership, will not happen by chance. It will have to be forged. Constructed. Nurtured. And tomorrow, I shall begin. "

Thomas lay back in his armchair, his head resting on the winged corner of the Chesterfield. He closed his eyes, trying to take his mind off the daunting task ahead. Not only had the experiment with the Wentworth lad failed, his earlier attempts to instil fortitude and intellect in women his own age had also failed. They left to be delectable wives of the great and the good instead.

> "I hope you're right, Thomas, about making this wife of yours," warned Daniel.

"As soon as we get back to Abingdon, upon their arrival, I shall observe them for forty-eight hours. Set simple tasks, challenges, and puzzles. Look at their strengths and weaknesses," he mused. "And from there, I can come up with a prescription to mould them into the philosophical partner I seek. Address anything that does not meet the standard, then propose to the stronger of the two girls, once they reach marriageable age."

"Yes, about the girls—what are you going to do when people notice two fillies turning up at a single man's house?"

"I shall merely tell those nosey busybodies that they are my domestic servants. Victor and his aunt both live at the house with me. There's nothing improper going on. They are not at my carnal 'mercy,' for goodness' sake."

"So why did you have to forge Wentworth's signature on the paperwork?"

"Details, Daniel, details. You always get bogged down with details, rather than getting on with 'doing'."

Astley was glad to be rescued from another savaging by the irascible Thomas when Victor reappeared. He decided not to ask what would happen to the girl who didn't rise to Thomas's expectations.

"Will that be all for the evening, Sir?"

Thomas glared at his valet until he corrected his form of address.

"Will that be all for the evening, Mr Thomas?" asked Victor.

"Almost. Tell me, Victor, what do you look for in a wife? "

"Well, I haven't snared a wife yet, but somebody who's still got all her teeth and can darn my socks will do. I like the idea of a simple, homely wife, but a little different from yours, perhaps, Sir? I mean, Mr Thomas."

"I think Mr Astley here dreams of marrying a risqué music hall star one day. Travelling around Europe and America with her, living the highlife, mixing amongst the upper echelons of society? Those with new money, not the old? Isn't that so, Daniel? "

"Well, I wouldn't say no if the opportunity presented itself," chuckled Daniel, who then swigged the last of his drink and then gulped it down his gullet.

"This book says that a rational approach to marriage is the building block of society, just as much as a household, Daniel. It is something to take seriously, not merely a refuge to encourage licentiousness and lewd behaviour, giving you carte blanche to mark some girl's card. Within my marriage, I shall apply the principles of Giseau.

There will be demarcated roles for myself as the husband and for my wife. Our partnership will be forged on strengths and weaknesses, and combining those character traits to create the most productive and pleasant household—"

"You mean your beloved can chop logs for you when you can't be bothered?" joked Daniel.

"Not at all," reprimanded Thomas. "How many times do I have to tell you that women are not innately feeble or delicate? They are merely made that way—if they choose to kowtow to society, with its poor education standards for the fairer sex and the frivolous expectations of the middle classes. But no wife of mine will fall prey to that."

"Are you hungry, Victor?" chirped Daniel, tired of Thomas's single-mindedness.

"Starving. I haven't really eaten much today, apart from a jacket potato from a street seller when I was waiting for Mr Thomas."

"Well, why don't we go out, go to the Eagle Tavern and have a look at some of these 'songbirds' that I'm supposed to be so fond of? Marie Lloyd might sing there. They do a slap-up meal. Then onto Wilson's, perhaps? Make a night of it, eh? How does that sound? "

"Rather good, Mr Daniel. Rather good indeed. "

"Right then. Go and get your coat. It looks like it's about to rain soon. Let's not tarry. We can always have a few drinks on the way there before the performance to dodge the deluge."

Ever obedient, Victor glanced at his master. Daniel noticed the valet's concern.

"Let's leave this bookworm here to his thoughts."

Thomas smiled, glad to be finally left alone. A night on the town with Daniel and Victor sounded exhausting.

"See you in the morning for breakfast, Thomas."

"Yes," he replied absent-mindedly, rereading the scene in the textbook where the hero asks his wife-in-training to row across a lake in a great storm as a test of her strength and courage.

*

The next morning, back at the mission, Sister Nancy had gotten to the girls in the tin bath and had scrubbed them clean. Their heads were inspected for lice with a fine-toothed comb. Thankfully, they passed muster.

"You won't need your missionary uniforms anymore, girls. I'll take those back from you. Reverend Bennett thinks these garments will be suitable."

The girls received two charcoal grey maid uniforms. They weren't as professional looking as the traditional black and white ones that the maids in Mayfair wore, but they were functional, clean, and comfortable.

"This looks like something a milkmaid might wear," complained Amelia as she held the fabric up against her.

"It's free, clean clothing, girls. Not a patch, stain, or repair on it. Do not be ungrateful. What did I tell you about ungratefulness? It's the most awfully selfish trait for a young girl to have. "

"Yes, sister," chorused the two girls with a sigh.

Lucretia put on the uniform. It felt more like a fancy-dress outfit than work attire. She looked at herself in the mirror. Her nerves bubbled up in her stomach and tightened her throat.

"Sister, I know nothing about a country household. All I know is that I live here, where we have our meals prepared for us. And we do seamstress work. I know nothing about laundry or polishing silverware or windows or anything like that! How am I going to cope?"

"Fear not. Sir Wentworth is going to provide a thorough education. He's a man of some substance and already has some domestic servants in his household who will be able to teach you the basics. I'm sure you'll pick it up very quickly. It's charring, not railway engineering, Lucretia."

"Stop being so defeatist, Lucretia," interrupted Amelia. "I'm sure we'll be fine. What's happened to your East End gumption? "

Lucretia ignored her.

"Where's our guvna's—"

"—Sir Wentworth's," tutted Nancy.

"Where is Sir Wentworth's house, Sister?"

"Abingdon, I believe."

"Where's that?"

"Not far from Oxford, near the university."

"How long will it take us to get there?"

"A good few days, I would imagine. You'll only be
able to travel twenty miles a day by coach, and it's
probably sixty miles. "

"I've never been further than half a mile from the
mission," confessed Amelia.

"You'll be fine. Now, stop fussing," cooed Sister
Nancy. "Sir Wentworth is going to be here at
noon, and you need to be ready, so look lively
now."

"Yes, Sister."

The two girls trooped back to their dormitory to collect
their meagre possessions and waited for the call to go to
the main reception to meet their new master.

3

THE RETURN TO ABINGDON

Tutting at the time, Thomas Beadle strode out of his hotel bedroom and knocked on the adjacent door like a gaoler waking an inmate with a morning bowl of gruel. The sound reverberated throughout the corridor, but Thomas didn't care what anyone thought or who he might have woken.

The entrance creaked open, and Daniel Astley's hungover face appeared at the small gap, one red-rimmed eye looking the visitor at his door up and down

" Look at the state of you," said Thomas, noticing poor Victor trundling up the corridor in a similar condition.

"It seems you two obviously painted the town red last night."

"Possibly," said Daniel, rubbing his forehead and wincing at every sound. "Come in."

"What, you're not packed? Victor's here to take your bag down—leaving my trunk unattended out on the street!"

Victor stared at his feet, ashamed that Daniel had led him astray. Astley made excuses.

"I'm double-checking I have not left anything if you must know. I hardly unpacked a thing—"

"—in your rush to get over to the Eagle yesterday evening, I dare say," Thomas sniffed.

A sheepish Astley fumbled around the room, checking his bedside drawers under his sheets and pillows, swallowing hard and looking rather peaky as he bent down to check under the desk.

"Better be quick. Victor is here waiting. Which means there's no one looking after my trunk!"

"Alright! For goodness' sake, stop nagging, man," grizzled Daniel. "There. Done!"

He threw his portmanteau at Victor like a rugby ball, who scurried off with it equally as quickly.

Downstairs, Daniel casually slid his room key across the reception desk, and the two men glided through the foyer along the plush red carpet and out into the bright wintery morning beyond. Blinking hard, the sunlight hurt Daniel's eyes. Victor held his hat brim down as low as it would go without it covering his entire face

With a crack of the reins, the carriage rumbled its way to the mission, the noise and the swaying doing nothing to help Daniel or Victor's alcohol-induced nausea and pounding headaches

*

In the echoing Portland stone interior of the Deserving Christian Women's Mission, both girls waited in silence. Every time the double doors swung open, their eyes darted towards them, then fell with a mix of disappointment and relief when they saw that the newcomer was not Thomas Beadle. Soon, the torturous cycle was over.

"Good morning, Sister Nancy," boomed Thomas, striding over, shaking her hand so firmly that her rosary beads rattled together.

"Sir Wentworth," she replied, pulling her crushed hand away.

"I trust Sister Nancy has explained everything, girls? It's time to go."

"Yes, Sir," they both chorused, feet rooted to the spot.

"Right. Come on then," he growled with impatience.

The girls flinched as he raised his arm in a symbolic motion. Swiftly, Beadle swept the girls towards the exit. They barely had time to say goodbye to Sister Nancy as he bundled them towards the waiting carriage.

"Go on, now. Hop inside. There you go."

It would be a tight squeeze to carry all the passengers. Thomas Beadle's legendary frugality meant Victor wasn't able to hire anything more spacious. While it might have been just enough for three people, four was going to be a challenge. For Beadle, travelling in more comfort than was strictly necessary was an avoidable extravagance.

For the girls, it was confusing that they had been told their new overlord was Sir Richard Wentworth, yet he also seemed to be referred to as Mr Thomas Beadle. They put it down to some finer aspect of etiquette they were yet to understand.

Cooped up, trying not to be jostled into one another, the journey was long and tiring. The wintery roads were in a terrible condition. Victor was worried that the carriage's iron-shod wheels would sustain significant damage as they navigated through the icy, deep potholes. The hire companies' repair bills were always extortionate if a vehicle was returned to them in less than perfect condition. Thomas would have had a pink fit if his jaunt to London cost any more, but there was little Victor could do to avoid the ruts. Daniel felt the carriage was cold and draughty, but at least it didn't leak.

They made a couple of overnight stops at coaching inns, with the two girls sharing a room. Out of earshot of their new master, they argued about everything: whose bed was whose, when to turn out the oil lamp at night, when to get up. There was constant rancour, which only abated in the presence of their fellow travelling companions.

Eventually, early on day three, an exhausted and relieved Victor steered the still pristine carriage into Thomas's country residence. The wheels creaked and crunched their way up the gravel drive. Up ahead, the impressive building had a Palladian air about it. The dark brickwork was decorated with a mass of creamy white windowsills and a matching Corinthian-columned portico, which positively sparkled in the bright sunlight.

"Well, what do you think, girls?" said Daniel Astley as the coach pulled up, and they could admire the splendour of Ashton Manor, their new home.

"I ain't seen nuffink like it," drawled Amelia.

"You haven't seen anything like it," corrected Beadle.

"Nah, I ain't," said Amelia innocently, thinking Thomas's comment was a question rather than a statement questioning her grammar.

Sensing that Thomas would lose his temper sooner rather than later, Daniel stepped out onto the driveway. Victor pulled back the oil skin that had been protecting their luggage and carefully passed each piece down to Daniel.

Burdened with several bits of baggage, like an overloaded packhorse, Daniel staggered his way towards the front door, which magically opened in front of him. Victor's perplexed Aunt Sarah greeted the weary travellers. Her wait to see what 'the girl' would be like was finally over. Except, when there seemed to be two girls, not one, Sarah's mouth fell open.

"I'll explain later," Daniel whispered close to her ear

"Come on now, girls. In we go." barked Thomas, making the same shepherd-like shooing gesture with his arms to hurry them along.

The entrance hall was dark and brooding, just how Thomas liked it. Only thin slivers of light passed through the half-closed curtains. Several pairs were drawn completely shut.

The dreary interior was not helped by dark oak panelling on the walls, eating up any light that landed upon them.

As their eyes adjusted to the gloom, the girls noticed shelf upon shelf crammed with curious curios and strange bric-a-brac.

"This way, ladies," urged Sarah as she escorted them to the parlour.

The parlour was equally foreign to the youngsters. Several dusty-looking stuffed animals adorned the mantlepiece. On a walnut occasional table was some sort of bird of paradise, perched on a palm frond, mounted in a bell-shaped glass case. Beside it was a small carriage clock in a matching case, ticking along rhythmically. Tatty looking armchairs surrounded the fireplace. The room's focal point was an exquisite oil portrait painting of an older man and woman, whom the girls correctly guessed were Thomas's parents.

"Sarah, will you show them to their rooms, please?"

"Certainly, Mr Thomas."

" Victor will sort out another bed later today."

The valet gave his aunt a silent huff as he wondered just how he would do that.

The girls' eyes stuck out like chapel hat pegs as they stared at their new surroundings. It wasn't exactly squalor, but it wasn't neat and tidy, either. They anticipated a lot of dusting and cataloguing lay ahead of them.

> "Go on then," he prompted again. "Unpack your things, girls. I want you back here at noon sharp. Is that understood? We shall begin your induction."

> "Yes, Sir—err, Mr Thomas," they said, correcting themselves again.

Sarah hurried the girls along down a long corridor towards the servant wing, not that Thomas considered his staff as 'servants'. The label was a hangover from when his mother and father owned the property, and it had stuck.

> "That'll be their first test, Daniel, seeing if they can manage to be punctual without anyone chiding them."

> "Really? I hadn't guessed," teased Daniel.

The two men went upstairs to the study, both keeping a close eye on the time.

> "I'm going to give them a puzzle first. Get a handle on their intellect. What do you think, Daniel?"

"I think you should let them settle in a bit first. They've never been out of Whitechapel, let alone to a countryside manor. I think that will be puzzling enough for them for now without you setting something deliberate to challenge their grey matter."

"I suppose," said Thomas begrudgingly. "Manual labour shall be the order of the day."

Daniel nodded as he ran his finger along the top of a book-shelf.

Sarah opened the door to the girls' room. It was much brighter than the hallway but smelled damp. Lucretia tried to open the window to let in a little fresh air, but, somewhat disturbed, she discovered the wooden frame was nailed shut. It looked rotten, and both girls hoped the nails were a makeshift repair rather than a sign that their room would soon become a makeshift prison. They turned to see there was no lock on the door. 'Another good sign', they both secretly presumed.

"How will we know what time it is, Sarah?"

"Good question. There isn't a clock in here, is there? I tell you what—I'll come and collect you. How's that sound?"

"Thank you," trilled the girls.

"I'll give you a minute or two to settle in. I suggest you unpack your bags promptly. I suspect Mr Thomas might come and check how organised you are based on how well you store your possessions."

As soon as Sarah had gone, Amelia flopped onto the one bed in the room, spread-eagled, commandeering it for herself like an explorer might plant a flag in some prime undiscovered land. Irritated, Lucretia put her things in the larger of two chests of drawers. The bickering was about to resume when Victor appeared. Amelia shot up from the bed like an engine beam.

"I expect you're quite hungry, girls," Victor asked rhetorically as he carefully laid a tray of fresh toast and marmalade on the bedspread.

Lashings of steaming hot butter had melted into the crisp surface, softening it. The perfume of the sweet citrusy preserve filled the air, banishing the smell of mould. It was simple but wholesome familiar fare, and the girls lapped it up. As they tucked into the snack, they still couldn't determine whether their current situation was a blessing or a curse. It certainly wasn't anything like the grinding domestic life they had prepared themselves for—so far.

*

In the parlour, Sarah appeared, brandishing a pot of fresh coffee. She earwigged in on the conversation.

"I must explain to Richard Wentworth what we've done, Daniel."

"Yes, you better had—before Reverend Bennett catches up with him for an update!" warned Astley. "Now, onto the legal contracts I have drafted for the girls. I appreciate that they've not yet signed them, but I think we should discuss the finer details before we cross that bridge."

"Will this take long?" whined Thomas, a life-long dreader of paperwork and administration.

"No, five minutes, at most."

Beadle pulled his best 'I hope so' face.

"It's not my fault we now have two girls factored into the equation, is it? We have no option but to revisit the terms."

Astley flicked through a pile of papers, scanning each one before settling on a sheet to discuss.

"Now, the basic principle was that a girl was to be apprenticed until she was of marriageable age. At that point, you would decide if you wish to proceed with the betrothal. Similarly, the girl would also choose if she wanted to proceed."

Daniel skimmed his finger along the page, muttering 'blah blah blah' as he mentally ticked off the clauses not needing revision.

"Yes, here we are. This bit will need work. If you choose not to marry the girl, you are to give her a one-off payment of twenty pounds. Also, you are to encourage her to start her own business, or else to offer her for marriage to a suitable suitor and to provide a substantial dowry. I suggest that at the end of the experiment, in the unlikely event that both girls prove unsuitable, they should both be given the same options?"

Thomas nodded enthusiastically, hoping the clause review would soon end and his moulding of the girls in earnest could finally begin.

"Moving on to the question of education. How do you see that—"

Before Daniel could finish the sentence, Thomas interrupted.

"—I've already decided. It's quite simple. I shall finalise the curriculum today. Then, first thing tomorrow, the girls and I will go to North Wales. I shall, of course, take Victor and Sarah with me to avoid any nosey parkers or naysayers suggesting there is any impropriety in my experiment."

"Wales?" said Daniel, stunned at the unexpected declaration.

Thomas sighed, frustrated that Astley had not yet mastered mind reading. Sarah made her way back to the girl's room, kicking herself that she could no longer listen in.

"The importance of being in North Wales is that it's a Welsh-speaking community. This means, of course, that they will not understand what's being said around them, and thus they cannot learn any bad habits or unhelpful ideas during their education.

"It seems rather drastic, Thomas."

"Can't be too careful," warned Beadle, as he peered through one of the curtain slits. "As you know, my mother was Welsh, and she ensured I had a reasonable understanding of the language. I know enough to get by. Furthermore, Wales will be good for evaluating their mettle. The harsh, windswept Snowdonian hills will be perfect for assessment."

"You mean you can test if they will cope as mountain maids? By Jove, Thomas, you are following Giseau's principles to the letter."

"I couldn't possibly say," said Thomas with a wry smile. "We'll soon find out if they can be self-sufficient rather than reliant on the trappings of the modern world."

Unlike Cragside or Waddesdon Manor, Daniel thought there were no mod cons at Beadle's manor house. Cragside had its own electricity generator, and Waddesdon recently had a shiny new elevator fitted to impress the Prince of Wales on his latest visit. Technologically speaking, Ashton hadn't moved on since a sundial was fitted in the formal gardens centuries ago.

"What if the girls try to escape this basic, backbreaking rural life?"

"They won't," said Thomas with utter conviction as he glanced at the carriage clock.

"Time's marching on, Daniel. Let's get these clauses redrafted before I announce that we will be leaving tomorrow."

Daniel took a clean sheet of paper and scribbled down the new terms.

"We can get the train to Lake Bala. I can't be bothered with the expense of hiring one of those blasted coaches again. Besides, it's so much more comfortable and efficient to travel by train."

Daniel agreed with the comment about the train. A couple of paces behind Thomas, he dwelled on the latest developments. Astley was unconvinced about the Wales idea and the change of plan to pick the strongest candidate from the two. It made him fear the girls might squabble for Thomas's attention. Beadle, however, seemed to be ecstatic that the experiment was underway as he swooped into the hallway as bold and determined as a hawk diving down to catch its prey.

"Ah, girls. A word if I may," said Thomas. "Let us go upstairs. There is something important I want to happen that requires your consent."

The word 'upstairs' and 'consent' terrified the girls, and they pondered what their strange master wanted them to agree to. Their relief was palpable when they realised he meant his study—and not his bed.

4

SETTLING IN

The girls had barely finished lunch when Victor reappeared, dragging a simple straw mattress behind him.

"I can't get a bed frame for love, nor money, I'm afraid—so one of you is going to have to sleep on the floor tonight."

The two girls looked at each other like angry duellists, wondering who would win the upper hand. Noticing the frosty atmosphere, Victor reassured them that he would resolve the matter as soon as possible. However, he neglected to mention it was likely that the bedding shortfall might only be resolved when they got to the cottage in Bala.

"And, er, Master Thomas says he would like you to come to the kitchen forthwith."

The two girls were still staring at each other, both vying to be 'top dog'.

"Come on," Victor snapped as he clapped his hands together. "You don't want to disappoint him on your first proper day of work, do you?"

"No, Victor," they whined without a hint of remorse.

"Once you get to know him, I think you'll find that master Thomas has a progressive view of the role of women. I've certainly not met a man like him in all my years on God's green earth. I think you've both fallen on your feet."

The girls looked unconvinced. During their time travelling in the coach, they had correctly surmised that Thomas Beadle was an odd fellow, with quirky dress sense and even quirkier opinions, but a champion of women's rights was not a trait they would assign to him. He seemed very controlling if anything. Victor tried to defend Thomas.

"I think our master thinks that the roots of education are bitter, but the fruit is sweet," the valet added with a smile. "And you must hang on for that fruit, girls, for I can tell you it's worth it."

The convoluted compliment was lost on them. Lucretia began stacking the tray with the soup bowls, welcoming the distraction. Victor tried again, this time being more obvious with his praise.

"No matter how frustrating Thomas can be at times, he does have people's best interests at heart. He just has a strange way of showing it. Certainly, took my Aunt Sarah and me under his wing when we needed help."

The girls looked even more confused. In the books they read and the discussions they'd had at Sunday school, the rigid class system meant English society was very much a case of 'us' and 'them'. There were no 'progressive' masters in this world, only entitled, selfish well-to-do folk who looked down on the likes of poverty-stricken orphans like them.

"Chop, chop!" barked Victor as he picked up the tray.

In silence, the trio snaked their way towards the study.

"In you go," he said, nodding towards the door.

Tentatively, Lucretia opened it and was instantly greeted by Thomas's voice.

"Ah, excellent. Girls, do come in."

Sat at the worm holed, grubby, the old desk was their new master. His elbows rested on a pile of papers, his fingers tightly interlocked. Daniel stood behind him by the window, taking in the view of the lush green Cherwell valley, a fine cloak of mist and a sprinkling of tall trees added to its rolling majesty.

"Now, before I allocate your first task for this afternoon, I feel I've been a little bit dishonest with you and my motives for bringing you here. Therefore, I must address the issue head-on."

The two girls looked perturbed, fearing what he was going to announce.

"You don't need to be afraid. Take a seat now, will you, and I will explain."

They planted themselves onto two plain wooden chairs in front of the ramshackle desk.

"Over the past few days, I hope it has not escaped your attention that I am not Sir Richard Wentworth—"

The girls had thought of nothing else but didn't want to admit to speculating about who he really was.

"—however, I am his close friend. Richard is fully aware of my actions. Indeed, I have struck a bargain with him."

Daniel turned to give the edgy trio a reassuring smile.

"Wentworth is a powerful industrialist, very well-respected in the community, and, more importantly, a happily married man."

Thomas relaxed a little, loosened his fingers and moved to sit on the edge of his desk, hoping he would look less defensive and more approachable. He wanted to be viewed as a man with nothing to hide behind, literally or figuratively.

"You see, for me to apprentice you from the orphanage. I had to impersonate a married man. There are strict rules about apprenticeships. As you may have guessed, I am a bachelor—,"

"A confirmed bachelor," added Daniel.

Thomas glared at him.

"Now, I believe that both of you have the makings of being a fine wife. You do want to be somebody's wife, don't you?"

The two young girls said 'yes, even though they weren't quite sure what being a wife might entail, especially to someone as eccentric as Beadle.

"Now, Daniel here is a lawyer. Everything, I assure you, is above board. He is here to act in your best interests."

"As well as yours, no doubt?" Lucretia snarled. "Thick as thieves, you two."

"I assure you, I am here as an impartial bystander," Daniel replied.

"Mr Astley has reviewed all the relevant family, employment and contract laws and has drawn up some papers. A contract that I will sign with both of you."

The girls were very much out of their depth by now, but, in the middle of nowhere, penniless and relying on the goodwill of four strangers, they were powerless to protest. They hoped things would make sense soon.

"Daniel has designed this agreement to protect your future—and mine. Quite simply, my plan is to educate the two of you in the realms of the household, academia, and the natural world. Given the start you've had in life, I expect this instruction will take a few years to complete. At the end of this training phase, I shall ask the stronger of the two candidates to become my wife."

Both girls baulked at the idea. For all his wealth, Thomas was extremely unattractive. His slovenly appearance resurfaced once he left London, and impressing Sister Nancy was no longer a priority. Neither girl wanted to be his wife, but neither wanted to be forced on the streets either.

"What about the other one, the one you don't pick? What happens to her?" Lucretia blurted out.

Thomas was about to lose his temper. Daniel put a steadying hand on his shoulder and took over explaining the finer points of the arrangement.

"I can assure you, the offer is as genuine as it is generous. You are under no compulsion to marry Thomas, merely to consider his proposal when the time comes. For the woman who does not become his spouse, she shall be granted the sum of twenty pounds."

This part of the announcement made both girls sit bolt upright. Twenty pounds would take years to earn by any other means.

"As well as the financial reward, there are two further options to consider. Firstly, Thomas will help the unsuccessful candidate to set up a business and be financially independent. Else, that woman shall be introduced to a suitable marriage partner, where he will also fund a dowry to make sure the match will be agreeable to the groom's family—you are, after all, orphans of no real pedigree or substance."

Amelia didn't quite understand the subtleties of the arrangement. Lucretia didn't care. All she heard was the mention of the sum of twenty pounds being given to her when she didn't marry Beadle, so she was quite happy to consent. 'I shall make sure I remain thoroughly repugnant to him. Within a couple of years, the money will be mine, and she'll be saddled with Thomas,' the scheming girl plotted.

Tired from the long journey and not wanting to show her ignorance by asking for further clarification, Amelia put an X on the paper next to Daniel's finger. Thomas was rather disappointed to see she was not able to write her own name. He had assumed the girls would be literate at least. Clumsily, the nervous girl dropped the fountain pen on the desk, leaving a string of inky-black splotches on his pristine blotting paper pad.

Lucretia picked up the pen and signed her name with a masterly copperplate flourish. The standard of her handwriting impressed Thomas, and he made a mental note that Lucretia might be the more intellectual of the two. He congratulated himself. 'Another bit of evidence gathered for my grand experiment.'

The two girls stood up in silence, reflecting on the implications of the contract they had just signed. Someone was going to be Thomas's cherished bride and the other foot-loose and fancy-free with the opportunity of a lifetime. Either outcome would be a step up for a lowly White-chapel orphan. The question was, who would get what?

The study door creaked open, and the soft noise of a swishing skirt filled the room. It was Sarah.

"Excellent timing," said Thomas with a grin. "Everything is settled here. Would you mind taking the girls to the kitchen and setting the first household task?"

"Certainly, Thomas. Come on, it's time to show us what you can do."

*

Later that afternoon, the two orphans were battling with a stack of copper pans that had been blackened with soot over the years. None of the pots in the mission had been copper, they had been made from cheap cast iron, so the girls had no prior experience to call upon.

They were not told how to clean the pans or where to find the right cleaning materials needed to bring back their gleaming shine. That was all part of the puzzle Thomas wanted them to solve. Furthermore, he ensured there was only one suitable rag for applying the Brasso, anticipating that the girls would have to negotiate and prioritise the work as they completed the task. Thomas thought they were the perfect conditions to assess their ability to plan, be respectful, and measure their productivity simultaneously.

Every now and again, he would waltz into the room unannounced to check on their progress, never uttering a word on whether he was pleased or disappointed with their endeavours.

The lack of resources, inevitably, made the squabbling flare up yet again.

"Why are you so slow," hissed Amelia, who had been twiddling her thumbs, waiting for her turn to use the rag.

"I'm not slow. I am thorough," replied Amelia before breathing on the base of a pan and buffing it furiously.

"You need to pull your weight, you lazy little madam."

Amelia snatched at the rag, tearing it out of Lucretia's hands, then ripped it into two tiny halves.

"You'll do anything to get your own way, you will, Amelia! Stupid cow."

Lucretia grabbed her half, coughed up a big ball of yellowy phlegm into it, and then, in a swift headlock manoeuvre, rubbed the rag all over Amelia's face. Then, like a pair of Cumberland wrestlers, a violent tussle ensued.

With a swishing of skirts, Sarah reappeared.

"You'd better not let the master see you behaving like that. How can you be so ungrateful?"

"Sorry, Sarah," muttered Amelia.

Lucretia, however, was quite happy to disappoint Thomas. Failing to meet his exacting standards meant a cool twenty pounds would land in her pocket. She gave some backchat to Sarah for good measure.

> "I don't see what the point of this task is anyway," complained Lucretia. "It's not like 'is lordship is throwing lavish parties, catering for the masses, is it? I would imagine the only houseguest he ever has is Daniel."

> "Don't be so rude," warned Sarah.

> "My point still stands," complained Lucretia. "The bloke's a weird loner. No wonder Thomas can't get a bird to marry him. He ain't right."

The cruel comment annoyed his loyal supporter. Thomas had been kind enough to keep Sarah and Victor employed when his father died, even though he felt 'servants' had no part to play in his own life, simply another extravagance in life he could easily do without.

> "You have been asked to complete a task. I suggest that you do as you're told," warned Sarah defensively. "I can assure you, life is much, much easier when you work hard and keep on Thomas's good side—rather than feeling his wrath if you laze and take his kindness for granted."

As Sarah left, Lucretia repeated the dressing down word for word in a mocking high-pitched voice. Amelia continued to hog the materials, refusing to share them with Lucretia. Just out of view, via the reflection of the kitchen door pane, a simmering Thomas observed the squabbling, the veins throbbing in his temples as his blood pressure rose.

He strode in once more and inspected the work. The girls fell silent.

"I thought you would have had these done by now?" he said, glancing at a clock on the wall. "It's been three hours now."

The girls stared at him.

"I suppose you're telling me this is good enough?" said Thomas, running his fingers along the surface of the bottom of the pan then staring at the sooty mark it left on his hand.

The girls said nothing, which riled him even more.

"Enough. The purpose of this task was to check that you could work together and quite clearly that is not going to happen."

Amelia looked down at the kitchen bench, ashamed:

"Sorry, Mr Thomas."

Beadle glared at Lucretia until she gave in and apologised.

"Now, go back to your rooms. I shall send Victor to collect you once I've devised the next piece of work."

He leant his head out into the hallway and bellowed for his trusty valet to come.

"Take these two ungrateful wretches back to their room," he snapped as he marched off towards the study.

Far in the distance, the door slammed shut into its frame.

"You've really got to knuckle down, girls," whispered Victor. "He's a fair man until he loses his temper. And then things aren't nice."

While Amelia heeded the warning and resolved to improve her behaviour, Lucretia was delighted she had managed to be a disruptive disappointment already, hoping that Thomas might pay a smaller fee, perhaps ten pounds, to be rid of her sooner rather than later.

Alone in their shared room, Amelia decided that life would be a lot more bearable if a truce was declared. She sat on the mattress on the floor and gestured that Lucretia could take the comfortable bed.

"Look, we've both been conned good and proper. Neither of us volunteered for this way of life. But things will be a lot better if we work together rather than fight, wouldn't you say?"

Lucretia stared out of the window, pondering what sort of business she was going to set up. Businesses with a woman at the helm were very much a rarity in 1890, and it would take some thought.

"Well, you must admit it makes sense?" Amelia prodded.

Lucretia turned to face her but still said nothing.

"Let's think about the good points of our situation, shall we?"

"I don't think there are any," Lucretia lied, as she imagined holding crisp pound notes in her hands.

"My initial assessment of Mr Beadle is that he is a wealthy philanthropic and open-minded man who seeks to nurture people. We would do well to impress him, wouldn't you say?"

"Impress a liar, who got us here under false pretences? Deceived Sister Nancy and the Reverend like it was nothing? He's a kidnapper to my mind!"

Amelia looked concerned. She'd heard tales of women being stolen by wealthy men and all sorts of terrible things happening to them when they were forced into brothels. Lucretia noted her worried expression.

"For the moment, we're being asked to do housework. But what if that changes—to more sinister duties, Amelia? Sordid, sadistic duties—?"

Lucretia let her voice tail off, pleased to see Amelia becoming overwhelmed by dark thoughts. Eventually, Amelia shared them.

"I still think we'll be safer if we stick together."

Lucretia nodded, with no intention of collaborating whatsoever.

As day turned to night, Amelia fell asleep on the cold thin mattress. Her roommate lay awake on the bed plotting, wondering how she could engineer Amelia's downfall—make things so horrible for her that she would run away well before she turned eighteen and never get a whiff of Mr Beadle's cash.

*

In the study, Thomas and Daniel were planning more of the girls' education, this time a task to test their physical resolve.

"We need to assess who is as tenacious as a Spartan woman," announced Thomas. "Fierce, independent, able to look after themselves while their warrior men were at war, as well as defend their townships from threats, should the Persian army see them as easy pickings."

"They sound quite savage to me," said Daniel. "I quite like my women with airs and graces. Delicate souls, fragrant, wonderfully gentle and feminine."

"You are entitled to your opinion, Daniel, and I am entitled to mine."

Victor appeared with a tray of tea and cakes.

"Is now a good time to mention we can't go to Wales tomorrow?"

"What?" yelled Thomas, frustrated that another bit of the experiment was proving troublesome.

"Well, there's talk in the village about a landslide near Crewe a couple of days ago. No trains running until Tuesday, I'm afraid. I've adjusted the plans to take that into account."

"Fine, fine. As you wish. And—er—thank you."

Thomas scratched a big line through the curriculum he had been working on and put his head in his hands. Training the girls was proving far more difficult than Giseau's book had suggested.

5

THE TRIALS BEGIN

"How do you think it's going to work, Victor?" said Astley as they shared a cup of char at the dowdy kitchen table. "It was a crazy scheme to start with. But having the two girls to contend with, well!"

"Quite," said Victor ominously.

"I just can't see him pulling it off. Not for years, I mean. He started off alright, just getting them polishing some pans, but I fear, soon, the tasks will become more challenging, more fraught— dangerous even. It's as if he's been possessed by the rules in that damned Giseau book. Common sense has gone out of the window."

"He's always been a man with a strong mind," agreed Victor, making the understatement of the century.

"Just keep an eye on the girls, will you? Try to curb his excesses with this experiment. I have to head back to London soon."

"Wouldn't devoting my life to plaiting fog be easier?" Victor added with a wink.

"Ha! You know him so well!"

The two smiling men slurped at their warming tea, then stared at the condensation dripping down the scullery window. Through the little rivulets of clarity, it looked bitter out that day.

Sarah had woken the girls at just gone daybreak, swishing the thick curtains open, letting the light flood in.

Bleary-eyed, both girls had suffered a fitful night. Amelia had been tossing and turning on the lumpy cold floor, and Lucretia gazed at the ceiling until the early hours, plotting how to extort the maximum amount of money from Thomas Beadle as soon as possible.

"Morning, girls!" she chirruped to raise them from their slumbers. "And how are we today, hmm?"

She didn't wait for a response.

"The Masters got another task for you," she said as she whipped the eiderdowns off the girls.

"Please not more cleaning," whined Lucretia as she pushed her arm through the sleeve of her woollen work uniform.

"Now, I understand this is a test that will be conducted outside."

Amelia looked at the ancient trees, bending and bowing in the face of a strong Northerly gale. Behind them, a slate grey sky threatened a downpour at any moment.

"If it's not cleaning, what is it?" demanded Lucretian.

"Everything will be explained by Mr Thomas. He's got it all worked out in your curriculum. All you need to do is be present and correct, girls. It's not a difficult concept to grasp. I shall come and collect you in ten minutes."

"Yes, Sarah," said Amelia.

Lucretia was as rude as ever and ignored the woman.

Downstairs at the grand entrance to the house, the heavy main doors had been thrown wide open. They swung wildly in the wind. Outside, Thomas was pacing in a long trench coat, the tail slapping behind him like flags on a ship's mast, his gloved hands clasped firmly behind his back.

"Finally," he bellowed as he saw them arrive.

He stormed over to the front door.

"Come on, I've been waiting."

Sarah gave the girls a light shove out of the hallway. The gravel on the drive yielded a gritty crunch under their boots. She battled against the wind to close the doors, glad to be out of the icy draught at last. She watched Thomas lead the girls over to a small wooden shed.

"Here, take these," said Thomas, handing each girl a battered old oilskin that belonged to his father's old gamekeeper.

Neither fitted the girls properly, but it provided respite from the worst of the weather at least.

"Good. Let's get going. It's going to take most of the morning."

What 'it' might entail remained a mystery. Beadle walked off along the gravel track, explaining nothing. The two girls trotted behind, pulling the oilskins tightly around them.

They followed a twisty footpath across Thomas Beadle's land. At the thick woods, they dodged a relentless onslaught of low hanging branches. Treacherous potholes that threatened to twist an ankle in a flash needed careful sidestepping. In the deep hollows along the route, many a muddy puddle blocked their way. It was slow going, and they only covered a mile in just over an hour.

Thomas kept turning around, checking on the girls' progress and gave them a stare if they fell too far behind. He noticed neither girl stopped to assist the other. Ever.

Finally, the weather began to break a little, and a small chunk of blue sky was just visible above the Oxfordshire valley.

Amelia hoped the sun would poke its face through the gap and offer some cheering warmth. The thinner of the two girls, she was frozen to the bone but didn't want to say anything. If she did, Thomas would have just told her to walk quicker to raise her core temperature.

Half an hour later, they found themselves staring into the depths of the River Cherwell from its waterlogged banks. In the shady patches under the trees, the grass by the river had a thin, delicate layer of frost on each blade. It crunched underfoot.

After picking a suitable spot to begin his address, Thomas pointed to two spots on the ground and huffed and puffed until they stood to attention before him, like soldiers on parade.

Thomas assessed the water, shoving his hands deep into his warm coat pockets.

"Have you ever heard of Sparta, girls?" demanded Thomas.

"Not really, Mr Thomas," said Amelia.

"Nah, course not," added Lucretia, in her best East End accent.

"Well, they were a hardy race of women, pertaining from ancient Greece. They were resilient. Brave. Fierce. Able to look after themselves, no matter what."

He picked up a sizable stone and threw it into the river. It sank out of trace with a thudding splash.

"You're going to go in there."

The water looked terrifying. Cold and fast-moving, the poor girls' dread worsened since neither could swim.

"That's bonkers," argued Lucretia.

"Not at all. Everything in the curriculum is meticulously planned. Nothing happens by chance around here. This will test your hardiness, believe me."

Amelia thought the experience might kill her, let alone test how resilient she could be.

"I want you to get undressed and in the water this instant."

Lucretia started to loosen the buttons of her oilskin, then her work uniform. Amelia felt very uncomfortable at the sort of a man being able to see more of her bare flesh that she might normally have on display.

"You can leave your undergarments on."

Amelia looked relieved. The girls stacked their clothes neatly, hoping the damp wouldn't soak into them. Stood with their knees knocking in their creamy white undergarments, thin blouses and frilled pantaloons that stretched down to their knees, they awaited the next instruction.

"Right. In you get," ordered Thomas.

"'Ow long will we be in the water?" asked Lucretia.

"Until I tell you the experiment is concluded. Quite simple. Now stop delaying, and let us begin."

Amelia took a few tentative steps towards the water's edge, the surface of some small icy puddles cracking underfoot as her bare feet landed upon them.

Lucretia was far bolder, keen to get the trial finished as soon as possible, a bit like ripping a plaster off in one go and planned to submerge herself in one fell swoop.

It would be Amelia who went first. She submerged her foot up to her ankle. Instantly, the limb felt like it had been hit by a hammer. She wanted to pull her foot out immediately, only enduring the agony for a second. It simply took too long for the relief of numbness to wash over her flesh.

Beadle was becoming frustrated. He marched behind and gave them a gentle shove so their centre of gravity would work against them on the slippy bank. Both girls' feet were soon submerged. Amelia gasped in pain. Lucretia swore like a docker under her breath.

Beadle's insistent hand remained in contact and pushed them further into the river. At that point, the Cherwell was about twenty feet across, so neither girl knew its depth.

The constant bubbling and bobbing of the surface made it impossible to see down to the riverbed. Then, as they took another pace, long slimy reeds reached out and enveloped each girl's ankles, like zombies reaching up from beyond the grave, making it hard to move. Then, mercifully, numbness finally began to take over, apart from the same agonising creeping line of coldness that travelled up their body as they eased themselves further into the raging river. Now, four feet from the safety of the riverbank, they were submerged almost to the knees.

"Lie down there," barked Beadle, fighting to be heard over the wind.

"What?" Lucretia demanded.

"Lie down in the water. I want you to be completely submerged apart from your faces. Do I make myself clear?"

The pain was excruciating. Amelia sat in the shallow water, her heart pounding with shock and her skin feeling like it was being stripped off her bones in one big sheet.

Thomas pulled his warm felt collar up around his ears, sheltering from the cold near a broad tree trunk. Stretching his arm with his palm towards the sky, he felt the first distinct splatters of rain. Curious, he examined the watery specks. 'It's not rain. It's sleet.'

"Come on, girls. The sooner you get started, the better. Fully submerge yourselves now."

As they complied, Amelia's teeth chattered like a trolley laden with cups and saucers. Lucretia put her lip between hers to silence them.

The torturous conditions made Amelia's mind wander to brighter times. She thought back to her time at the mission, how she decided their dormitory in the orphanage wing had been freezing, but she'd never experienced cold like this before.

Looking at his watch, Beadle made a note of the time.

"Good. Stay like that for an hour. That should do.

'An hour!' thought Amelia. It felt like a lifetime away. She was desperate to get out but feared the wrath of Thomas if she disappointed him. On the other hand, she was sure a creative mind like his could work out an even worse punishment than the current ordeal if she tested his patience.

Thomas began quoting philosophical methods at the girls, hoping to evaluate their powers of recall and reasoning when learning under duress.

"Pay attention, now. I shall be testing you when we get back to the hall."

Lucretia rolled her eyes at the suggestion. There was no way she was going to remember anything. It was up to Mr day to decide if that was deliberate or accidental.

Finally, Beadle called time on the experiment. Both girls rolled over onto their fronts and crawled out as relieved as a shipwrecked castaway scrambling onto a lush tropical island. Amelia was so weak she could barely stand. Lucretia seemed to have fared better and was quickly on her feet and marching towards her oilskin.

"Well done, girls. That's the first physical test passed. Compared with yesterday's dismal performance, this was stellar."

Their wet clothes clung to their rounded curves, but unlike other men, Beadle noticed not.

Amelia pulled the oilskin around her like a cosy cocoon. A little plume of steam escaped through the gap at the collar into the cold, crisp dawn.

"Let's walk quickly now. You'll soon warm up."

Like a sergeant major leading his battle-weary infantry back to barracks, the girls staggered behind all the way to the hall.

The bedraggled youngsters made a beeline for the front entrance, desperate to warm up inside.

"Not that way, you foolish things," Beadle piped up. "You'll drip all over my marquetry floor tiles and warp them. "I'm not most house proud of men, but I'm not fond of costly water damage."

Sarah was horrified to see the girls, now white as ghosts, not a drop of rosy blood to flush their skin, no noses rosy from the cold.

She glanced over at her nephew Victor in concern. He shook his head, despairing at the obvious harshness of the physical test Thomas's young wards endured.

"Please make the girls a drink, Sarah. They performed well today and deserve a small reward."

"I'm going to go upstairs and set them a test on Descartes' model of the essence of existence. We were discussing it earlier, weren't we girls."

The little baffled voice in Amelia's head was not so sure.

With a hot drink inside them, the girls' mood lifted a little. Sarah took their clothes and helped to dry them in front of the roaring fire in the parlour. Once returned, the garments smelled smoky, but at least they were warm and dry.

"The master's ready for you in his study," said Victor.

As soon as they were changed, the girls were ushered upstairs.

"Have you read many texts, girls?" Thomas enquired, skimming his finger along the crackled leather-bound spines of the nearest bookshelf.

"We had a few library donations at the orphanage," Amelia replied. "But I must confess, I never really got the hang of reading, if I'm honest. I did try. But the penny didn't seem to drop."

'I like her honesty. A fine quality in a wife,' Beadle noted mentally.

"And you," said Thomas as he held his mouth inches from her ear.

"A few, if you count reading the Penny Dreadfuls," she blurted out proudly, knowing it was going to rile Thomas even more.

"Penny Dreadfuls? Good grief! Whilst I applaud your desire to entertain yourself with the written word—reading rags like those, well, it just rots the brain."

"Why don't you choose one to read, Miss Amelia?"

The girl's keen eyes skimmed the lettering that adorned the spines. There are a lot of words she didn't recognise. She suspected most of the books were in Latin. The thoughts of reading a book in English felt challenging, especially if she couldn't even write properly. Tackling something in Latin was utterly pointless. Then, she saw a book by Dickens.

"I'll take this one, Mr Thomas," she said confidently, please that she could at least decipher the words on show on the shelf, if nothing else,

"I'll take this one," said Amelia, boldly picking up Isaac Newton's 'Philosophiæ Naturalis Principia Mathematica'. The only thing she recognised was the author's name. Everything else was baffling. 'Perfect,' thought Lucretia.

"Sit there. I want you to read two pages and summarise what you have learnt. Then we will do the philosophy test I promised."

Amelia groaned silently. Lucretia gave nothing away in her body language. Before they could even start to read, Beadle attempted to cram their heads with more of his views.

"I don't normally think that being bookish is a worthwhile endeavour." said Daniel, "Books are like learning from a long-dead tutor. Don't you think it's far better to receive some instruction from a fellow human describing the wonderful principles that govern our world? And then going out and observing them first-hand."

The girls hoped he had finished his lecture, but he hadn't.

"Why read a book about flying a kite when you could make one? Take it out on a bracing day like this and feel the string tugging against your finger as the fluttering shape in the sky tries to fly away. That is learning about kites. Looking at a simple rhomboid shape on a page teaches precisely nothing. Do you see what I mean, girls? Experience builds knowledge, not being a bookworm."

"You've got a lot of books for somebody who doesn't think they're any good," teased a confrontational Lucretia.

As Beadle ignored her crass comment, she looked at the strange symbols making up the formulae on the page of Newton's Principia. She was as clueless as the first western explorer attempting to decipher hieroglyphics in Luxor temple.

"The same is true of dancing, needlework, playing an instrument. The learning comes not from reading but from doing. So, we shall be doing a lot of 'doing,' girls. And of course, I shall have my eye on you to see who is the most adept at turning their hand to new mastering subject matter."

When he quizzed Lucretia about her book text.

"Well, a geezer called Newton wrote it. But that's about as far as I got."

Thomas was livid that the flippant girl had obviously picked a book that was beyond her comprehension.

"Do you think it is acceptable to take board and lodgings from me and completely disobey my polite instructions? You have invalidated this part of the experiment, Lucretia. What were you thinking?"

"Dunno," she replied, like a little tearaway pickpocket on the fiddle in Borough Market.

The blood drained out of Beadle's lips as he pursed them close together to avoid shouting at the girl. There was no point bullying either of them to be a better wife. Firm yes, dictatorial no. They had to want self-improvement for themselves.

Amelia mentioned her text was about Mr Scrooge. She struggled with the next bit as she traced her finger along the sentence.

"And? What else?"

"He was a c-c-cur-cummud-gee-on," she stammered.

"Curmudgeon. What an excellent word, Amelia. Yes. Scrooge was indeed a curmudgeon," said Thomas, offering a rare few words of praise.

Given how a task as basic as reading was panning out, Beadle decided to give up on the Descartes quiz. The girls just didn't absorb information as readily as he had hoped.

'A less rigorous syllabus will be required for some time,' he lamented. 'Else, they will not take a single thing onboard. Absorbing new knowledge and mastering practical skills is more important than reaching a finishing post that lay years ahead of us. And I think I will need years to instil the necessary know-how into their thick little heads.'

"Be off with you. Get some food. You are dismissed."

After a simple evening meal of water leek soup and stale bread rolls, the girls decided to get a good night's sleep.

There was no question of swapping places. Lucretia commandeered the comfortable bed for herself again. She flapped the eiderdown over her head and turned her back on Amelia, left once more to battle with the lumpy straw mattress on the floor.

Downstairs, a grizzly Thomas sought out Victor.

"Please tell me that blasted landslide's been dealt with?"

"It has. And before you ask, I've got five tickets for the morning. I meant to tell you but with you being busy all day—"

"Excellent. Well then, Victor, my man, early to bed, early to rise."

"Right you are, Sir."

"Five thirty."

"What!"

"Let's prepare for departure at five-thirty in the morning. It's going to take us quite a while to get to Oxford station, and we have several connections to navigate on our way to Bala."

Victor groaned.

"Yes, Thomas, of course. I'll let my aunt know to wake the girls in good time."

"No matter what, I can always rely on you, my good fellow. What would I do without you?"

"Probably exactly what you want, you stubborn old pain in the neck," joked Victor quietly, hoping that Thomas didn't overhear his musings.

6

THE TRAIN TO WALES

The early morning train journey to Wales was smooth and swift, yet the girls felt uneasy.

The rhythmic puff of the engine pulled the carriages through deep valleys, past deep forests, mining towns, and old villages that had sprung up alongside canal basins a hundred years ago.

Victor looked at his pocket watch.

"Another hour, and we'll be there, I reckon."

The girls nodded, not taking their eyes from the window for a second. The countryside was different again from the Chilterns. Slate grey rocky outcrops loomed above them, looking as impenetrable as the walls of the Tower of London.

After disembarking at Bala, Victor organised an old cowman with a cart to transport them to the old dairy cottages that had belonged to Thomas's family for generations. The walls were adorned with posters written in Welsh. Unlike the music hall posters back in Whitechapel, the girls couldn't read a word of these, but they couldn't quite understand why. The letters looked similar, but the meaning was unfathomable.

The porters clanked along with their wheeled trolleys and began unloading the goods from the train. The noise and bustle meant the girls didn't notice the different language they were yet to understand.

The cart Victor organised trundled along a long ramshackle single-track path for what felt like an eternity. At the front was a sure-footed horse nodding along in time with its steady gait. Next was a hunched-up old man with wispy grey hair that reached his coat collar and a jacket that looked three sizes too small. He grasped the reins with his leathery arthritic fingers, the joints more swollen than broad beans in their pods. At the back, on the hard wooden flatbed, five grimacing passengers were jostled with every pothole and stone the cartwheels careered over. Clutching at their luggage, they feared it would slide off into the mud at any moment.

The cold wind whipped off the Irish Sea and cut through their clothes. They would all be grateful to get inside into the warmth. Then, finally, the cartman stopped. Victor hopped down and collected the luggage.

"Show the girls their room, will you, Sarah?" groaned Thomas, grabbing the cart's handrail and swinging a leg down.

As their tired, gritty eyes focused on their surroundings, two quaint semi-detached cottages came into view in front of them. The walls daubed with so much thick white-wash, the rough stone underneath was now pristinely smooth. The bottom foot of the wall was different, splattered with mud and farmyard muck, a casualty of the wet and stormy climate. The roofs were thatched with golden straw rather than covered with the world-famous grey Welsh slate.

"Hwyl fawr," said the cartman, with a toothless smile and a wave.

The two girls looked at each other and shrugged their shoulders, wondering if they were the same words used on the posters.

With a crack of the tatty leather reins on the back of his horse, he was gone.

Thomas pushed the creaky door of the left-hand cottage open. The girls peered into the gloom of the place that was to be their third home in just over a week.

Against one wall was a traditional wooden Welsh dresser with four plates proudly displayed behind a thin rail on the top two shelves. Eight hand-painted floral enamel mugs hung on the hooks underneath, the decoration similar to that found on a canal barge. The rest of the cabinet's contents remained a mystery behind the closed cupboard doors.

Someone had obviously prepared the cottages, as there was some dry wood and a little bit of newspaper, ready to start a fire. Stacked in a recess in the wall was a good stack of dry logs.

"Why don't you light that, Sarah? It will warm us all up a treat."

"Right you are, Mr Thomas."

Taking a small flint, Sarah's numb hands launched some sparks at the kindling. She blew at the orangy glint in the hearth, and soon the fire took hold.

"This room will be yours," said Thomas, going into a small annexe off to the side.

Two small wooden beds, barely three feet wide, were covered in a coarse grey sheet topped with another blanket made with colourful crochet squares. Both the mattresses and pillows are made of horsehair stuffing and felt quite plush to the touch. Compared with the rest of the austere landscape they found themselves in, at least their bedroom was welcoming.

"Choose which bed you're having. They're both the same, so I'm not expecting any squabbling," Thomas muttered, his voice trailing off.

"Your bags, girls," said Victor, leaving them at their bedroom door.

Back in the tiny front room, Sarah sat on a small low stool, staring into the golden glow of the fire.

"You hungry girls?"

"Starving," came the eager reply.

"I'll see what I can rustle up for us."

The girls pushed their bags under their chosen bed and flopped down, exhausted. Their eyes were just beginning to gently drift closed when, louder than a foghorn, the word 'girls' was barked into their room.

"There's vegetables to be peeled. This is no time to rest!"

Like two zombies, they stood up and shuffled behind Sarah as she led them to the other larger cottage. On the table were some wizened root vegetables and a large clay jug of ale. The ensemble was completed by a mound of pearl barley in a bowl. The ingredients, like their accommodation, were frugal but would do the job to fill their rumbling bellies

"Go to the pump and fetch some water, Amelia, would you?"

As her arms pumped the stiff lever, behind her, she heard a terrible noise. Startled, she dropped the pail in terror.

Equally startled were six hissing geese that were dashing around the backyard, flapping their clipped wings, trying to escape but failing. Like the buildings, their plumage was a perfect snowy white. Then, in a defensive movement, the angry birds moved en masse towards her. Amelia shrieked. Hearing the commotion, Sarah opened the window to investigate.

"They are only geese, Amelia, not ghosts! Surely you've seen them at Smithfield market. That's the meat market near Whitechapel, isn't it?"

"I only saw dead ones that were left on a cart. I never saw them running around like this. It's like the devil's possessed them!" she said, shooing them away.

"They'll calm down soon enough," chuckled Sarah. "Hurry up with that water."

The geese decided the stranger in their midst wasn't a threat after all, and they went back to filtering the water in the deeper farmyard puddles with their orangey beaks. Amelia picked up the pail, stepping on the hemline of her skirt as she lent down. Irritated by the mistake, she stared at the thick brown stain and sighed. 'How do such simple little creatures manage to stay so pristine? I look like I've been dragged through a hedge backwards in five minutes flat,' she lamented.

Sarah and Lucretia giggled when Amelia returned, caked with mud and her hair tumbling out of its bun.

"It's definitely different, country life, but you city girls will soon get used to it."

Sarah turned her attention to Lucretia, who had barely scraped a square inch off the parsnips she'd been given. She tutted with disapproval. The laziness in that girl was quite astounding. It was obvious she had no inclination to do anything whatsoever.

Sarah reprimanded her for her poor work ethic yet again. Thomas overheard and mentally made a note of the criticism.

By the time everything had been washed and prepared, the range had heated up nicely. Sarah scooped the vegetables into a cast iron pot and put them on top of the stove. She added enough ale to cover everything and left it to simmer. It soon bubbled away merrily like a witch's cauldron.

"That's our stomachs dealt with," Thomas announced, rubbing his hands together eagerly. "Now it's time to think about our minds. Come on, get your coats."

He tapped his foot impatiently as the girls scuttled next door.

Thomas gave no indication where they were going as he strode off down the lane, expecting the girls to follow suit. For all they knew, they could be walking for ten minutes, or ten miles. After the long yomp to the river for yesterday's physical ordeal, they hoped it was the former, not the latter.

Thomas's long legs picked up the pace, and the girls became breathless, trying to keep up. There was no respite until Thomas stopped to knock at a cottage close to the eastern shore of Lake Bala. Peering over the dry-stone wall that surrounded the tiny dwelling, it was obvious it belonged to a carpenter. There were a pair of trestles stacked high with thick planks of wood.

Thomas opened the garden gate and beckoned the girls through. Their eyes darted everywhere as they assessed the unfamiliar place. Amelia would have toppled backwards into a deadly saw pit had Thomas not grabbed her by the elbow first. He panicked and barked at her:

> "Be careful, Amelia. This is a workplace, not some pleasure gardens to stroll around in your Sunday Best. Keep your eyes peeled, please."

Seeing a rugged young man approach them, Thomas loosened his grip on the girl and walked to greet him.

> "Daffyd Beadle, my good fellow!"

> "Cousin, what brings an Oxford man like you to Wales?"

> "I—we—need to build a boat."

> "I see," said Daffyd, baffled as he eyed up the two young girls in toe.

> "Yes, I fancy supplementing our diet with some fish. A man needs more than watery vegetable soup three times a day," said Thomas with a chuckle. "Grilled brown trout is much nicer, especially if you've caught it yourself."

Daffyd laughed at the way Thomas felt he always had to justify a little luxury in his life. It suddenly dawned on him why the girls were with his cousin. 'So, Tommy really is going through with his experiment, the old goat,' he mused with a smile.

"What do you know about boatbuilding, girls," asked Beadle, even though he knew the answer would be 'absolutely nothing.'

Silence. He changed tack.

"If I were to say to you, 'Archimedes principle', what would that bring to mind?

"Archie?" asked Lucretia. "The only Archie I know is Archie Rice, the one-legged dancer down Wilton's Music Hall."

Thomas clenched his jaw tightly shut to contain a string of expletives threatening to break free and made a mental note of yet another gap in the girls' understanding of the world around them. He looked around for a piece of driftwood and a stone to teach them about buoyancy to address the problem.

Lucretia was thoroughly disinterested in his academic babble, preferring to cast her eye on Daffyd's muscular arms as he worked. Amelia, however, soaked all the information up like a sponge. Suddenly, eyebrows aloft, Beadle stared at the two girls, with high hopes they could now answer his question, but he was greeted with silence. His face turned thunderous.

"So—?" he demanded again.

"So, our boat will float because it's hollow—and air is lighter than water," said Amelia, tentatively.

Thomas jumped for joy. *'Finally, some progress.'* Hearing the tense exchange, Daffyd brought over one of the toy yachts he'd been making for his son.

"Thanks," said Thomas, grabbing at the tiny hull. Our boat will be like this but better, girls."

He dropped the little vessel into the water, and it bobbed around then settled on the surface.

"Don't tell me, Thomas. We're going to be teaching them how to build their own fishing boat?"

"Indeed, we are. Daffyd here is a skilled woodworker," he said, leading the girls towards a smaller workshop at the back of the property. Amelia flinched.

"Oh no! Quick get a bucket! The sheds on fire!" yelled Amelia, unable to understand why Daffyd and Thomas were so nonchalant.

"It's not on fire, you daft apeth. That's steam, not smoke," Thomas laughed. "Daffyd steams the wood, so it becomes supple, and he can bend it to shape. This is called a steamer box."

"Oh," said Amelia, blushing.

Daffyd opened the door to the steamer box, and a huge billowing cloud of wet air puthered out. He disappeared into the vapour but returned seconds later, wielding a plank.

"This bit's nearly ready," he said, flexing it before them.

Amelia thought Daffyd was like a modern-day alchemist, turning the stiff plank into a malleable material.

"I'll make you some wood, and then you can make a start on that boat of Master Thomas's. Should be ready in a day or so. In the meantime, take some of my rosemary to put into that watery soup of yours," said the carpenter.

"I think they serve thicker gruel at the workhouse." lamented Thomas.

"I thought you were a man of simple tastes? No fine living for you, Mr Beadle," teased Daffyd,

"I am a simple man!" protested Thomas, "But that doesn't mean to say I'm happy with bland. Come on, girls. We have a big day ahead of us tomorrow."

"What are we learning then?" said Lucretia thinking she'd better show a little bit of interest.

"Rest your little heads tonight. I think you've learned enough today. Reflect on what you've been taught. We should start early in the morning."

They marched back uphill to the family cottages, arriving just as it began to rain. The mucky farmyard around the cottages squelched under the foot. The geese ran for shelter in their little house by the dry-stone wall.

So hungry with all the hiking, their stomachs thought their throats had been slit. The vegetable pottage, watery as it may be, smelled wonderful.

"What time do you call this," said Sara, as some bowls clattered into place on the table. "I'll see that the girls are all right in here, then I'll come and serve up your meal."

Thank you, Sarah," said Thomas as he disappeared next door.

Sarah flexed her muscles, laid the heavy cast iron pot on the table, and then ladled out the soup. It wasn't anywhere near as watery as they were expecting after Thomas's complaining earlier. In fact, it was bordering on wholesome and nourishing.

"You all right, girls?"

"Yes, thanks," said Amelia before she leant forward and tucked into the rest of the food.

Sarah joined her master next door, finding him chuckling. "I think I put the fear of God into them, teaching them about Archimedes' principle," he said, jabbing at his soup with a thick hunk of bread.

"I've never met someone like you, Thomas," said Victor. "I mean that."

"Good. Most people fall short of their potential."

"What's the plan for the girls tomorrow?" asked Sarah.

"We've got a busy day, fun-packed from dawn till dusk!"

"Really?" said Sarah.

"That's if you call slaughtering geese 'fun,'" said Thomas. "Time for a bit of butchery knowledge, I think. Can't live on fresh air."

"Hmm," said an unconvinced Sarah.

Next door, after dinner, the girls turned out the oil lamps and collapsed into bed. Amelia did her best to remember what she'd been taught while Lucretia dreamed of Daffyd. 'He's almost worth forgoing the money for!' she thought as she wondered if eloping was an option.

7

LIFE IN BALA

The wintry sun rose around eight o'clock. Sarah had already got the girls up by bringing breakfast to their room—a thick slice of bread, each slathered with rich farmhouse butter.

"Thomas will meet them outside as soon as you are ready."

Both dressed in their basic farm girl uniforms, hungrily, they chomped on the meal. The wet, muddy yard of the previous evening was now crisp but slippery, coated in crunchy white ice. He wasn't at the front of the cottages, so the girls skidded and lurched their way to the backyard. Over by the far corner with the shelter for the geese was Thomas. He was resting his hands on a makeshift wooden pen. Ensnared within it were two of the beautiful white creatures.

"Today's lesson is self-sufficiency, girls. It's all very well and good helping yourself to pre-prepared food off the plate, but that food has to come from somewhere. And today, we are going to learn where that is. I don't suppose you had much opportunity to deal with livestock at the mission?"

"Livestock?" Lucretia piped up.

"Yes, things like this: animals, birds?"

"No. We did see the odd horse off to the knacker or Barry McGinty and his vicious German Shepherd wandering about on rent day—"

"—there were pigeons, plenty of them," added Amelia. "But nothing like these birds."

"Hmmm," sighed Thomas, keen to move onto the teaching now it was clear the girls were clueless yet again.

"Today's lesson is going to focus on how we turn these flapping squawking noise machines into delicious meat."

"We are?"

Lucretia used to baulk at killing mice that wandered into their dormitory. Sister Nancy would order her to dispatch it swiftly with a heavy boot. She had no idea how to tackle a goose.

One of the birds in the pen reared itself up and flapped its wings furiously. The wingspan was almost four feet across. The prospect of wrestling with one looked quite daunting.

"Now, it's important to handle geese safely and humanely, girls. Although they don't pose as much of a threat as a swan, of course, they still need careful handling."

The strange philosophy graduate, so often awkward with people, seemed able to charm the bird into submission in seconds.

"It's important that you have control of the head to avoid getting bitten."

"Bitten?"

"Yes, these geese have small, serrated teeth. Here, watch this."

Thomas hopped into the pen and waited for the geese to calm down. Then, quick as a cobra strike, he grabbed one by the neck, a couple of inches behind its eyes.

"You see, just like that. Take care not to apply too much force."

Thomas seemed to have the same talent for controlling animals as the Pied Piper of Hamelin. He applied a small amount of pressure, and the goose sat down obediently folding its wings back up, allowing Thomas to get closer. The other bird was the exact opposite, doing everything it could to get as far away from the intruder as possible. Beadle seemed unconcerned.

"Now, once you have hold of the neck, girls, you slide your other hand under the body. Be quick about this. Otherwise, it'll start to struggle again, then firmly clench the legs between your outstretched fingers like this."

With his palms in a bowl-like shape and his fingers splayed, he was able to trap the legs. He brought his forearm down towards his body, and the bird was soon trapped yet quite relaxed as it was handled.

"You just need to take control, see? Show them who's boss."

The bird was hemmed in between his torso and forearm, pinned by the head and legs, yet it seemed quite calm. It was then that Thomas struck. He reached into his pocket for a metal rod and swung it firmly and carefully towards the bird's skull before it noticed its head was free. The blow was so severe that the bird fell immediately unconscious, but, as planned, it was not enough to kill it. Thomas prodded at the head. The limp neck fell down and swung by his arm. He swung his legs over the side of the pen and walked towards the girls. Both of them took a step back.

"Come on, girls. This is no different to a lion taking down a gazelle. This is how the world works. There are hunters, and there is prey. And we human beings are the hunters of the farmyard animal. It's all perfectly normal."

As the girls looked on, it looked anything but 'normal'.

"Now it's unconscious. We need to slit its throat or break the neck to ensure immediate death. This is the most humane way of doing it. It's not easy to ensure an effective blow to the skull with manual stunning like this. You have to be committed. Whilst we are hunters, we are also humane."

Both girls felt their stomachs do a somersault. Lucretia forgot about her long-term self-interest and focused on looking away.

"How are you going to learn if you're not looking, Lucretia? Look at me!"

"Yes, Master Thomas," she said quietly.

Amelia was completely lost for words.

"I prefer not to slit the throat. It limits the chance of disease transmission via bodily fluids. If we dislocate the neck by rupturing the spinal cord, breathing quickly stops, but we have not spilt blood."

Thomas looked to check the girls were still following the basic principles. He wasn't sure they were but pressed on anyway.

How do you think we should do the dislocation?"

The question was met with silence.

"Let me rephrase the question. Do you know how a man is hanged? Was there ever talk of one of those ruffians at Newgate at your mission?"

"Yes, all the time," said Amelia, looking at the bird, wondering if it was going to come round since the discussion was taking quite some time.

"And?" questioned Thomas.

"When they fall through the trapdoor, the noose breaks their neck."

"Exactly, Amelia. Well done."

"Farmers do the same but in reverse."

Nothing was any clearer despite Thomas's elaboration.

He walked over towards a strange tripod with a large, galvanised cone riveted to the top of it, then dangled the goose's head into the metal mouth. It was just big enough to accommodate the body. The bird's floppy white head and neck appeared out of the bottom of the cone. He took a set of metal pincers off a nail in the wooden pen. With the head locked between the two prongs, with a quick snap with his arm, there was a sickening crack. As the bones gave way, Thomas loosened the prongs and the birds. The neck swung like a pendulum.

The barbarity of taking a life like that sickened the girls. They both stared wild-eyed at Thomas, but he was not going to be put off by their lily-livered city girl outlook.

"You, come and check the neck's broken," he commanded, beckoning Lucretia over with a few jabs of his index finger

He grabbed her hand and ran her fingertip over the neck bones as he bent the head awkwardly. There was a clear, clean break, with two jagged ends of the spine poking out towards the skin. The plumage and skin ran softly over the spot, disguising the severity of the injury.

"Feel that?"

A pale-faced Lucretia nodded.

"Put your finger near the eye socket, see if it flinches."

Lucretia gulped as the lifeless eye gave her a look like she had betrayed it herself.

"And the eye, is the pupil dilated?"

Lucretia leaned in as close as she dared and then nodded. Thomas swept the bird away, knocked on the window and bundled the lifeless bird through it to Sarah.

"That's the first one done. The girls will bring you the next one once they've prepared it."

The girls looked at the one remaining goose in the pen, which was strutting about pecking at the mud from time to time, unaware of what had just happened to its fellow feathered friend. Thomas pushed them both towards the pen. Suffice it to say, distressed and sickened, the girls' attempt was nowhere near as polished.

"It will get easier. Everyone has to start somewhere," said Thomas, chivvying them along.

"I don't want it to get easier," murmured Amelia, the thought of practising umpteen times filling her with dread.

Amelia was nearly in tears as she walked towards Sarah, the dead bird lolling in her arms. She looked at it, its dead, lifeless eye staring back at her, taunting her that she had betrayed the bird in some way. She felt guilt, shame, despair. Life in the East End had been tough. But this rural life, this hands-on brutality, was very challenging.

"Would you like any soup, girls? There's a bit left over from yesterday," said Sarah.

They both shook their heads, swallowing hard, their focus still on the dead geese lying on the floor by the range.

"I'll show you how to get rid of the plumage, gut the bird and prepare the meat to make a confit."

"How can it be comfy?" whispered Lucretia.

"Confit. Preserving it in solidified fat in a bowl."

Plucking and gutting sounded equally grim tasks. Unsure when their next meal might be and not relishing the prospect of eating some of the goose they had just slaughtered, they were glad they were able to force down their portions of bland pottage after all.

The afternoon was spent at Daffyd's woodworking workshop, learning how to saw and plane wood.

"Spartan women would make repairs to their forts, make their own carts. That's why we're doing this, girls. Remember, burying your head in a book will do nothing to teach you how the real world works."

"But we don't live in ancient Greece. We live in
Victorian England, Master Thomas."

He ignored Lucretia's protestations, reasonable ones for
once.

Later, he inspected their hands, noticing they were sore
from clutching the tenon saws. Blisters were forming near
the base of their thumbs from using the files for hours. He
was pleased neither girl had complained and had priori-
tised getting the job done ahead of their own personal
needs. Stoicism was one of Thomas's highly prized traits.
The gentry girls he had chased in the past always fell
short in that respect. He thought they were delicate little
wallflowers, delightful to look at, but would collapse in an
instance when faced with the mildest overnight frost.

Daffyd kept a close eye on them to ensure that they were
not cutting the precious softened wood too short. As
Thomas looked on, he watched Daffyd teach the girls how
to lay their carefully prepared planks against the central
wood of the keel. Both pieces fitted perfectly. Lucretia's
heart fluttered as Daffyd's hand brushed against hers as
they aligned her plank.

"Excellent work, girls," said Thomas, as they
strode back towards the cottage once more.

After quite a gruelling day, the praise was welcome. The
warm fuzzy feeling was soon to fade, however. When they
got back, Sarah was preparing the first of the two geese,
plunging the bird into a huge bubbling cauldron of hot
water, pressing it down with the soup ladle from the day

before. After about a minute, she fought to get it out and lay it on the table.

The skin of its beak was blistering, and the eyes were cloudy and congealed, no longer staring at their murderers. Once more, the girl's stomachs lurched. The scalded head thudded onto the table. Sarah got stuck into removing the feathers, her hands making a rhythmic ripping sound as each quill left the pinky-red flesh. Then the disembowelment began. Amelia wanted to wretch. Lucretia focused on the long game and the promise of money when she was dismissed as unsuitable for the curious man who had taken them in.

"They've done well today, Sarah. Give them extra rations, extra butter on that bread to go with some more soup. We've learned a lot today, haven't we, girls?"

They nodded, without confessing, mastering today's skills would have not been their chosen subjects if they'd been given a free choice.

"Have you ever salted meat to preserve it, girls? We could make a start tonight with the offal."

"No," came the exhausted reply.

8

FURTHER EDUCATION

Over the coming weeks, the girl's relentless education continued. There were flora and fauna lessons out on the Welsh hills. There was a visit to the Menai Straits to see Brunel's magnificent suspension bridge and discuss who should fund civil engineering projects. There was repairing the dry-stone walling around the cottage, fixing the cart's axle when it developed a fault.

The scope and scale of the experiment were exhausting, and things came to a head one day, down at the lake. After yomping like squaddies down to Daffyd's workshop, the wheels were set in motion for an event that would ultimately scupper Thomas's experiment.

Thomas ran his fingers along the smooth varnish on the wooden rowing boat. Its construction had taken the trio a couple of weeks. The finish was bone dry. The boat was finally ready to sail. Beadle slapped his hand against the upturned hull.

"You've done well here, girls. We've made an excellent craft."

The few words of praise cheered the girls, Amelia more so than Lucretia. Daffyd trotted to his workshop and picked up a special wooden trolley. He set it down by the boat, by the middle of the keel.

"Ready?" he said, grabbing the edge of the hull with both hands.

Carefully, everyone grasped the boat, and it was manhandled into place, resting on the trolley. In unison, they held it steady on the wobbly little platform and wheeled it down to the water's edge.

Thomas looked at the girls expectantly, hoping they would notice something was missing, but they didn't.

"Can you get us the oars, please, Daffyd? We won't get far without them."

"Right you are, Thomas," the carpenter chuckled.

Together, the trio took the heavy boat off the trolley like nurses sliding a casualty off a stretcher, communicating by feel and eye.

It landed gently on the gritty ground with a soft, controlled crunch.

"Right, you two get in, and I'll push us off from the side," said Thomas before resting the oars inside the little rowing boat.

The two girls look terrified. Although they lived near the Thames at Rotherhithe, it was such a busy stretch of commercial waterway, there was no chance of women using a pleasure boat like this. This would be the first time they'd been in a boat in their lives.

One girl got in at each side, and the boat rocked gently as they transferred their weight. It felt decidedly unsteady. After the experience in the river a few weeks earlier, they were petrified of open water, especially since neither of them could swim.

Quick as they could, they steadied themselves by flopping down onto the wooden bench at the back of the boat, then held on for dear life.

Thomas gave the boat a great shove forward until there was just enough for the water to lift it slightly. The tiny vessel began to glide gently on the surface. He hopped his legs in, and he took his seat, then reached for the heavy wooden oars

Soon they were ten feet from the shore.

"She floats like a dream, Daffyd," yelled Thomas.
"And look at this. She's completely watertight."

Bobbing about proudly in the water, they'd all done an excellent job of making her.

There was a clunk as Thomas put the oars in the little retainer hooks at the sides, and he began to heave. Steadily, the little boat made its way further into the lake.

"Time for geography refresher, girls. How big is Lake Bala? Either of you remember? We did mention it over dinner last week."

"Four miles long by half a mile wide," volunteered Lucretia

"100 feet deep," Amelia added nervously.

"Yes, excellent. Now, I explained that glaciers make lakes in this area, but there is a bit of folklore about this place and how it came into being. Would you like to hear the tale?"

Rather than dwell on the thought of 100 feet of water beneath them, both girls welcomed being entertained by Thomas.

"Tegid Foel, a Welsh prince, had a fine palace here in Bala. He lived a life of opulence and excess. He was known for his cruelty and greed, and he oppressed his people. When his first grandson was born, he decided to throw a lavish party to commemorate the occasion. He invited all the important princes in Wales and beyond, as well as his entire family. They say that a man is known by the company he keeps, and many people refused to attend the celebration because they did not want to be associated with this cruel and barbaric prince."

Thomas looked over his shoulder to check his course, then continued.

"Unfortunately, like attracts like, and the banquet was still attended by a number of powerful men of questionable character and behaviour. Tegid had hired Wales's best harpist to entertain his guests. While he sang his songs and played his harp, the wine flowed, and the guests indulged in all manner of excesses, oblivious to him. Surprisingly, he thought he heard a quiet voice behind him whispering in his ear while he was playing. It happened several times before he realised the voice was saying, 'vengeance will come!'"

The girls' eyes darted around, looking for birds.

"The voice startled him. The musician looked behind him to see a small bird perched on an open window, staring at him intently. 'Vengeance will come!' chirped the bird, then motioned for him to follow."

"What did he do?" asked Amelia.

"The man decided it was time for a break, so he went outside, carefully setting down his harp, and found the bird waiting for him by the door. They walked up the hill over there."

Thomas loosened his grip on the oar and pointed up to a high point up above.

"When the harpist awoke, he looked out from the hillside and was taken aback to see how the landscape had changed. The valley was now completely submerged, and the palace at Bala was nowhere to be found. The young man noticed his harp while floating on the water near the shore of the new lake. He managed to retrieve it by wading into the freezing water. He looked around for the little bird that had saved his life, but there was no sign of it."

Thomas grabbed the oar and straightened the little boat as it bobbed about close to the middle of the lake. The girls imagined the stone towers and turrets of a fairytale castle beneath them.

"Although the harpist was unable to see the bird, he expressed his gratitude and returned home, grateful to be alive and relieved that his precious harp had been returned safely. He realised that higher powers were involved in the flooding of the town and his survival. In a show of thanks, he dedicated his singing and playing to them. Tegid Foel and the evil princes who drowned had brought it on themselves and paid the price for their wickedness. The few survivors established a new town on the lake's shores, which evolved over time into the modern town we see today. According to legend, there are nights when the lights of the ghostly palace glitter beneath the surface of the lake."

The small waves making a regular 'slap slap' sound against the varnished hull were accompanied by the rhythmic splash of the oars. Thomas saw the boughs of the trees swaying in the breeze. The wind was picking up and whipping through the long, narrow valley.

"See, rowing is easy, girls," said Thomas. "Who wants a go?"

The trees at the lake's shoreline now looked like tiny toy ones surrounding a posh girl's doll's house. The further they got from land, the more anxious the girls became. Lucretia dipped her fingertips into the icy dark water and quickly pulled back.

"Amelia, how about you?" Thomas suggested, knowing neither girl would volunteer.

She gave a nervous smile and a nod, knowing saying 'no' would achieve nothing. With very unsteady movements, Thomas and Amelia swapped places. The boat pitched and yawed in the water, with the girl flinching each time it lurched. With a sigh of relief, she took her place at the slippy varnished seat by the oars.

Like a coxswain on a Viking warship, Thomas bellowed when to take a stroke. She soon got into the flow of rowing and even enjoyed it a little. She looked over her shoulder every now and again to check that her course was straight and true.

After a good thirty minutes, it was clear that Amelia was beginning to tire. Thomas suggested that the two girls should swap. They both got to their feet. Fretting about standing up, Amelia forgot to secure the oar on the left-hand side. As the boat rocked, it slipped away into the water.

"Look what you've done, you stupid girl!" shouted Thomas. "Reach for it before it floats away."

Amelia tried to kneel down, thinking she would feel more secure as she reached overboard. Lucretia was intent on taking the rower's seat. As the two girls negotiated their new positions, a large square wave came in from the side. The little boat wasn't designed to be hit side on so forcefully. The bow was supposed to cut through the water, not the gently curved sides. The left-hand side of the boat was lifted out of the water, threatening to capsize at any second. With Lucretia and Thomas more towards the right of the keel, the little boat didn't stand a chance.

In an instant, it was flooded and began to sink. Unable to swim, with their legs tangled in the thick woollen milking maid uniforms, the girls began to panic. The little rowing boat began to float down into the gloom, but the girls couldn't see for the splashing as they fought to keep their head's high. The cold water shock had taken their breath, and both had choked on some water when they were first submerged.

Choking, panicking, terrified, there was no way that Thomas could calm them down. All he could do was hope they would quickly exhaust themselves, so he could get close enough to hold on to them.

In desperation, he yelled for them to hold their breath to make them more buoyant, and it seemed that helped a little bit. Thomas bitterly regretted not making a life-ring. *'Schoolboy error!'* he bemoaned. *'If they could have just clung on to something, the girls would have been much easier to assist.'*

Lucretia coped better than Amelia, whose head was barely above the surface of the choppy water by now. With the weather worsening, the waves were a couple of feet high. Thomas was finding it difficult to keep his eye on both girls, and eventually, there was nothing he could do but jeopardise his own safety to rescue them.

He came up behind Amelia and grabbed her maid's uniform by the scruff of the neck, desperately trying to dodge her flailing arms.

"Calm down, Amelia, I've got you!" he yelled as he dragged her towards Lucretia. "Calm down! I'll get you back to shore. Calm down!"

Neither girl was listening, and it was only exhaustion that would finally make them comply. With all three of them lying on their backs, Thomas did all he could to keep their heads above water as he frog-kicked his legs towards the shore, hoping that going with the strong wind and waves would make the struggle to terra firma easier. He didn't care where he landed as long as he did. His lungs and thighs burned with the exertion.

As the girls adapted to their situation and began to trust Thomas would keep his word, they could at least kick their legs to help the trio get back to safety.

They crawled over the stony shoreline and collapsed, coughing and choking, barely alive.

Daffyd had been watching the scenario unfold from the shoreline. His boat was out of action, so he had done the next best thing and brought his cart along the little country lane on the lake's western shore. Soon he was with them.

He tipped the cart, helping them ease their way onto it. He grabbed onto the sopping wet survivors and hoicked them to safety.

"Hang on tightly, now. Spike and I will get you back as quick as we can."

He worked his horse hard to get them back as quick as lightning. Drenched, all three of them were shivering uncontrollably, the wind chill making them colder still.

Daffyd shouted to his wife they were back. She had been putting wood on the fire, doing her best to help her husband with the rescue mission. She looked out of the window and saw the three ghostly white figures lying on the cart. The fire would not be enough. She quickly gathered all the blankets off their beds and brought them into their little front room as Daffyd helped the three weaklings into the house.

"Take all your clothes off now," ordered Elsie. "It's the only way you'll get warm."

Even though their lives were in danger, the two girls were deeply embarrassed at the thought of getting undressed in front of strangers. In the end, their sense of self-preservation quickly overtook any feelings about morals and decorum. The two men looked away to protect their modesty while Elsie enveloped the girls in a blanket and sat them on a sheepskin rug by the small hearth.

The two men got changed, keen to get out of their soggy clothes. Unlike the two men, the orphans looked. Morality went out of the window again. Having never seen a naked man's body before, the two girls couldn't help but look, pretending that they weren't, of course. Elsie was too concerned about everyone's welfare to notice.

Lucretia's head was turned by Daffyd, unperturbed that his wife was in the same room. Amelia glanced at Thomas, the curious man who had just saved her life. Although he was harsh and difficult, there was something about him that drew him to her. Although the circumstances under which he took the girls under his wing was unprecedented, sometimes, it felt the most natural thing in the world.

It took a good couple of hours for the girls to warm through and to get their clothes dry. Thomas had warmed himself up by borrowing some clothes from Daffyd and running back up the hillside. Victor encountered him as he sprinted up the little lane to the cottages, on his way back from some errands in Llanberis.

"Quick, unload the cart and let's get down to Daffyd's. It's the girls."

Victor did as he was told, and the cart clattered speedily down the hill, almost out of control. Once more, the girls found themselves on the back of a wagon. Everyone travelled home in silence, wondering how a pleasure trip in a boat had turned into a perilous fight for survival.

9

SOMEONE MUST STEP IN

Sarah was furious when she saw the condition of the girls. Worried about where Victor had got to, she was staring out of the window, going mad with worry, thinking he might have had an accident or been robbed. Seeing Spike's nodding head appearing above the dry-stone wall, she dashed out of the cottage to greet him, then noticed the three others lying flat on the wagon. Both Amelia and Lucretia were pale, their lips blueing and fighting a hacking cough.

> "Heavens! What's happened? What on earth were you thinking, Thomas? Look at them! They're barely alive. I understand that you want to test them, really, I do. But this has just gone too far!"

Victor scooped up Lucretia, now barely conscious, and carried her to her bed. Thomas lifted Amelia by the arm, laying the limp limb over his neck then raising her up. As the weight was taken off her feet, they dragged behind her, lifeless, like tin cans on a string behind a wedding carriage.

The water had damaged their lungs. Retching often and coughing constantly, they were still very weak from their watery ordeal.

Thomas buzzed about Sarah, trying to explain and offering assistance, but she batted him away like a wasp.

"Do you want anything to eat, girls? Build your strength up, a hot meal, maybe? You can't have eaten since breakfast?"

They both groaned at the thought of food and shook their heads.

"Can you get me a bucket," whimpered Lucretia between coughs, the phlegm building up and bubbling in her lungs.

" Of course, my dear," she said, giving Thomas an evil look that meant 'don't just stand there, you get it!'

When he returned with an empty, dusty coal bucket, she snatched it off him in temper, angry that he hadn't even rinsed it. But Thomas was filled with remorse. It was his fault the girls' lives had been put at risk, and he knew it.

"You get some rest now. Take as long as you need."

Sarah didn't care if she got into trouble with Thomas. It was time to speak up for the girls. The experiment had gone far enough. It might have been a nice idea to rescue some orphans from the mission on paper, but it was a living nightmare in practice. She could no longer watch them suffer.

After mopping their brows with a clean cloth and rinsing the coal bucket, she carefully closed the door and let the girls have some rest.

In the other cottage, Victor and Thomas sat in silence, knowing that Sarah would give the master of the house the third degree. *'And quite rightly so!'* Victor thought.

"We will have no more of these wild and wonderful experiments Master Thomas."

He got ready to speak, but she cut him off dead.

"Not even when they're stronger. They've had weeks of intensive instruction. They might be making progress, but at this relentless pace, I can't stand by and watch it happen. They're fifteen-year-old girls, Thomas, not warriors or physicists or anything else you want them to be. There's plenty of time for them to adapt to your way of thinking. Let them rest. For all your talk of morals and ethics, yours, quite frankly, have deserted you!"

She stormed to the cooker and put the pan on the range with an almighty clatter, making the two men jump.

"It's soup for tea again. The goose pate's all gone, and you don't deserve the confit today, with your behaviour. If you want something else, go and get a meal at the Red Lion Inn in the town. And don't think of asking Victor to take you down there, either."

Her tirade turned into angry muttering as she gave the broth a stir.

Thomas drummed at the table with his fingertips. The 'tap tap tap' irritated the other two. He was obviously plotting something, and probably not what they wanted or expected him to do.

In reality, he was nervous. He'd had a lucky escape that afternoon. 'What if someone died? It would have been my fault' went round and round in his head. He knew that Sarah was right, but he didn't want to acknowledge that. Fidgeting was a way of easing his conscience. At least he didn't have to say anything or admit he was very much in the wrong.

"Fine! Have it your way," Thomas hissed, hoping not to show he was wracked with guilt. "They can rest."

He picked up his thick woollen coat and left the cottage, slamming the door behind him.

Victor shuffled in his seat.

"Don't you dare give him a ride to the Red Lion!" Sarah fumed.

Victor's forced compliment that 'the soup smells nice' fell on deaf ears.

Thomas wasn't seen until the next morning. He hadn't gone out to the inn. His appetite had deserted him too. He'd hiked up to the high point by the lake, hoping when he came back down, his life would be better. Sheltering in a ramshackle disused shepherd's bothy, he reflected on how the experiment was going. Did he have the stomach to continue with it? Or, like all his previous betrothed maidens had, was it time to give up on this strange idea of the perfect marriage? In his pocket, he ran his fingers over Giseau's book, wondering whether to read it or burn the damned thing for warmth.

Thomas wasn't the man to shirk away from difficulty, and he didn't want to make a snap decision. Yet he felt if he took his time to mull things over, Sarah would make the decision for him and somehow help the girls escape somewhere—anywhere, as long as it wasn't with a menace like him.

There was nothing stopping her from finding Richard Wentworth and telling him that the experiment got out of hand, that it had failed, just like it had with Wentworth's son. If Richard found out, he would put a stop to it too. Since he was the man on record who was supposed to be in charge of them, he wouldn't want his name splashed in the papers if one of the girls were to die. They wouldn't be out of the woods for quite some time, so severe were their breathing difficulties. Who knew how things might turn out?

As dawn broke, Thomas returned to his cottage, only to find Sarah and Victor were missing. Seeing their coats on the rack, he knew they couldn't have gone far. There was only one place they could be, and that was next door.

The girl's annexe door was open, and there was a voice talking in hushed tones, but it was neither of them. It was Victor, talking to his aunt.

"I can't believe how much they've deteriorated overnight," he whispered. "I'm terrified one of them might—" he croaked, too emotional to face the truth.

Thomas tiptoed towards the room, so he could listen in better.

"Look at Amelia," said Sarah. "Her skin is still bluish, and her abdomen is all swollen. Before she fell into that deep sleep, she was complaining of chest pain. You could see she was struggling. And Lucretia, well, I had to empty that bucket quite a few times, yet she'd barely touched any of the food I left for them."

During the night, Sarah had gone to check on the girls. Amelia tried to sit up and eat a little bit of food but had some sort of seizure and fainted shortly after. When she came too, she was drowsy and lethargic and wouldn't answer when her name was called. The only sound in the room was two sets of rasping, wheezing and tortured breathing. It was a stomach-churning sound, even as Sarah went next door to continue her vigil over the poor things.

"I could strangle that, Thomas! There was no need for them to go out on a windy day like that. What was he thinking, Victor?"

"I don't know. Maybe it just got worse while he was out. You know how changeable the weather is here."

"Stop trying to defend him. These girls are defenceless. They have no way of telling him that enough's enough. So, we're going to have to step in."

Then, Thomas gently pushed against the annexe door and gave a look to say that he would comply with Sarah's suggestion. Exhausted from a sleepless, guilt-wracked night, he was stunned to see the girls and the change in them. The pink, rosy cheeks and soft curly hair had left them. They were now pale, and their hair was matted and stuck to their heads. How he wished they would be bickering again, and Lucretia was giving him her trademark back-chat.

"I'll let them rest," said Thomas. "You're right."

The girls got worse before they got better, and at one point, it was touch and go for Amelia, who didn't rally as quickly as Lucretia despite faring better to start with.

As the girls grew stronger. The arguments resumed.

"It's all Thomas's fault," said Lucretia. "This stupid experiment of his to find a wife. There's no wonder he couldn't find one the normal way. I don't think it's got anything to do with his expectations. I think it's more of a case that he's cruel and heartless."

But it was different for Amelia. She couldn't help but think back to the connection that had formed between her and Thomas when he'd saved her life. Without his heroic efforts, she would be dead. And much as he was irritating and selfish, he had been her saviour. He had picked her first, so surely that meant she was his favourite?

"Look, give him a chance. I'm sure he'll see the error of his ways and tone things down a bit? Do you really think life in the mission was any better?"

Lucretia didn't respond and turned her head towards the opposite wall. All she could do was think about running away. *'Perhaps I could stay with Daffyd? Be a washerwoman or seamstress? It looked like they had a spare room. If I did some housework, maybe I could stay rent-free?'*

The plot to escape quickly fleshed itself out. From there, she would save enough money to get the train back to London, and get some common lodgings at Jimmy McGinty's place, ask about the pub for work. Anything was better than being held captive in the cottage in Wales, in a land full of people who spoke a strange language and barely knew she existed.

On the final day of their recuperation, Lucretia made up her mind. She was running away, and that was that. 'In the morning, I'll be gone. They'll pull back the covers, and there will just be some pillows under there, not me. In the morning, I'll be gone.'

That evening, Thomas met up with Victor and updated him on his progress.

"I've been in touch with one of Richard's connections. A woman who's his wife's milliner. She says she'll take Lucretia on as an apprentice."

"That's wonderful. Very kind of you," said Victor, pleased there seemed to be a way forward at last.

"Yes, her sullen and confrontational demeanour means that she can never really be the wife I'm looking for."

His selfish comment irritated Victor, but Thomas redeemed himself.

"I'll just give her ten pounds since she's leaving the process early. Perhaps one day, she can set up a shop of her own. I'll tell her in the morning. She's still resting, I believe."

"What's going to happen to Amelia?"

"I don't know," said Thomas. "She seems more obedient, more accommodating. And I think she might one day be the woman I'm looking for. But I won't know yet. There's still a long way to go."

10

10

THE LATE NIGHT FLIGHT

In the dead of night, after hours of lying awake mulling over her limited options, Lucretia decided it was time to make her escape.

"Amelia! Amelia! she whispered.

There was no reply. *'Excellent.'* Stealthy as a prowling black cat, Lucretia swung her legs over the edge of the bed, hoping the rickety bed frame wouldn't squeak. Carefully, she took one of her pillows, plumped it up, then put it in the middle of the bed. That was the torso shape made, but what about the legs? She knelt down and looked under Amelia's bed, then carefully teased out her carpetbag. There was barely anything in it, but it had just enough bulk for her needs.

The bag was laid next to the pillow, then Lucretia carefully covered everything and arranged the folds to make the lumps look as lifelike as possible. As she admired her work, her heart nearly stopped. Amelia became restless, moaning loudly as she turned over. Lucretia darted into one of the deep shadows, fearing Amelia would get that sixth sense that someone was watching her and wake up.

Amelia's bunged up nose meant her mouth gave a few light putters as she breathed out. She was definitely asleep again.

Lucretia tiptoed towards freedom, closing their bedroom door quietly behind her. Every second would count in the morning. If she was intercepted, then who knows what Thomas might do. His behaviour had become more extreme and erratic the longer the quintet lived in the cottage.

Sarah didn't know exactly where the two orphan girls had come from, but she was quite sure their masters wouldn't have sanctioned the treatment they were getting.

Something stopped Lucretia from running down the lane. A small golden glint on the windowsill of Thomas's cottage caught her eye. *'A candle? Someone's there!'* She hid to one side of the window frame, working out what her next move should be. Then it came to her. On closer inspection, the glinting object was Victor's precious pocket watch, a gift from Thomas. A wicked smile filled Lucretia's face. *'That little trinket is my meal ticket out of there—it's the answer to all my woes.'*

It was a wonderful bit of unexpected good fortune. She racked her brains, trying to remember one of Reverend Bennett's long sermons about the sin of stealing and how thieves used 'fences' rather than pawnbrokers to shift their stock. She wasn't sure what a fence was but figured a few questions in a few rough pubs, and she would soon put herself in the picture. *'What a stroke of luck. I can buy myself a little bit of freedom and be free of this hellhole.'* She gave a silent laugh. The change of events had been sudden, but within seconds she had planned her next move. If Lucretia had one talent in life, one thing she had mastered more than anything else, it was, without doubt, self-interested plotting and scheming.

The old plan, of throwing herself on the mercy of Daffyd telling him *'you and Elsie really did need an unpaid charwoman'* or trying to get a job as a chambermaid at one of the lakeside hotels, was thrown out of the window.

There was a tremendous flash of light, followed by the long rumble of thunder, so loud it was as if the earth and everything standing on it were giving a dying shudder. The cottage door opened. There was a voice heading towards the backyard.

"Oh, Spike, what's up, lad? Come here."

'Victor!'

The horse was terrified, pacing up and down as far as his leather tether would allow. Victor patted Spike on the neck.

"I kept telling Thomas we needed to build you a shelter. He's such a bleedin' cheapskate. Making you stand out here in a tatty old blanket, it's not right. I could throttle him at times. Silly old curmudgeon."

The horse whinnied, his hooves clip-clopping from side to side as he pulled his head up and away from the wall.

"Calm down. You'll hurt yourself yanking at your bit like that. There, there, now. Easy boy."

Spike was having none of it. Anxiously, he pawed at the floor with his front right leg. Lucretia ducked down and crept past the window, desperate to get the watch before Victor came in from the storm. If he was up, he might have woken Sarah. *'What if she's making a cup of cocoa to ease them back into their slumbers?'*

"Would you like a sugar lump, Spike? I can go and get you one? A cup of hot sweet tea always makes me feel better. You love a sugar lump, don't you fella?"

Another burst of thunder and lightning terrified the beast even more. Victor held the horse's head still and hoped Spike's clod-hopping hooves would not crush his feet.

"I only thought we'd be here a day or two, but it seems Master Thomas has other plans."

Lucretia edged her way towards the door. Observing Victor comfort his beloved Spike, she was confident he was lost in his own little world.

Inch by inch, she moved her head past the edge of the door frame, biting her bottom lip. She expected to hear Sarah's voice at any second. Lucretia had never felt lucky in life, and she hoped fate had stored it all up for this moment. The poor horse tried to rear up in fear each time a huge rumble of thunder passed overhead. She scanned the small front room. There was definitely no one there. Both bedroom doors were closed.

'Go!'

Within moments, the pocket watch was gone from the windowsill, and Lucretia swept out of the room, pulling her dark grey shawl over her head. Just as she left, she grabbed one of Thomas's two waterproof coats. *'That'll do nicely.'* She tiptoed away at first, not looking behind her, then ran as hard and as fast as her legs would carry her, only glancing back once to see she had not been spotted. With jubilation, she noticed finally she was free of the torment that had stalked her since she left the mission.

It was one of those nights where, even though the cloud was thick, the bright full moon just had enough strength to light the way. The lightning gave way to torrential rain, but Lucretia didn't care. She would have skipped with delight if the road wasn't so rutted and potholed.

Her mind looked to a new brighter future. Her right hand fumbled with the cold, smooth watch safely stored deep in her skirt pocket. She sang a few music hall ditties as she paced down the road. 'Won't be long until the first train, then I'll be out of this hell hole.' Then, she stopped in her tracks, as if she had hit an invisible brick wall, a wall of realisation. *'What if the watch has an identifying mark? What if I can't shift it?'*

She scratched her fingernail over the back of the case. It stuttered over a deeply engraved pattern. *'Damn and blast.'*

Pulling out the watch, in the gloom of the faint moonlight, she looked to see what the design might be, praying it didn't mention Victor, Thomas, or anyone by name, for that matter. Relief flooded her when it appeared to be some sort of swirling spiral of decoration. However, she was mistaken. It wasn't a pattern, but an inscription written in Greek:

> *'It is better to have a friend in times of need than money.'*

'Maybe I won't take it to the pawnbrokers. And I can't risk finding a fence. I need to shift this before Thomas catches up with me. Perhaps a porter at the station will have it? They need to know when the trains are coming in. Get a good spot by the first-class lounge and carriages. If I hang around till the end of the day when they've earned more tips, surely I'll get enough to buy a ticket back to London overnight with a few bob left over.'

If only Lucretia knew it read: "It is better to have a friend in times of need than money."

The rain was collecting in the ruts, the puddles making the terrain hard to distinguish. The mud sucked at her boots.

> *"I can try my luck at one of Jimmy McGinty's lodging houses until I get myself straight. If all else fails, well, I'll just have to take my chances back at the mission. Let them know they were duped by Thomas, and I'll tell the press. Might even cadge a few free nights.'*

The watch felt expensive, and Lucretia licked her lips in anticipation. She allowed herself a moment to dream a little more. After years of no control in her life, she was on the cusp of independence. She closed her eyes with delight, but that would be her undoing. She veered very slightly to the left. Her toe caught on a kerbstone poking up out of the mud. She tripped. Startled, she opened her eyes and tried to regain her balance, but it was too little too late.

Her centre of gravity was thrown, and the treacherous road surface thwarted her attempts to right herself. Her hip landed just beyond the edge of the road, and inevitably, she rolled down towards a short, rocky ravine that ran alongside the road.

Falling like a child ragdoll down the stairs, she rolled, bumped, bounced, crashed, collided, and finally collapsed. In agony, she found herself at the bottom of the narrow little ravine, completely out of view. She felt her lower body washed with icy water from the little stream that flowed into the lake. Dazed and afraid. Lucretia knew she had to get back up the ravine, or onto the bank at least, out of the freezing water. She did everything she could to drag herself back up to the road to safety.

Soon, it was breakfast time at the little cottages. Sarah opened the girls' door with her usual cheery greeting.

"Morning. The food's ready. Your favourite, Lucretia, egg and soldiers. We're celebrating. Today is going to be an incredibly good day,

Missy. Mr Thomas has some excellent news for you."

In the low morning light. Sarah couldn't quite make out what was going on, but she knew that something was wrong. The celebratory feelings melted into concern. She set down the tray on the dresser. A bleary-eyed Amelia sat up and stretched her arms above her head.

"Finally, a good night's sleep," Amelia cheered.

"That's good, dear," said Sarah, not really paying attention.

Eager to find out what was causing the sense of foreboding, she whipped the curtains wide open, and the overcast light fought its way into the room. As she turned back towards the beds, it was then she noticed. Lucretia hadn't moved a muscle.

"Come on, girl. Time to shake a leg," said Sarah in her commanding voice.

The realisation came quickly. Sarah pushed the lump under the covers and instantly knew it wasn't a person. Pressing the flimsy pillow, it squished down flat. *'That ungrateful little madam has made a run for it! After everything Thomas has done for her too.'* Amelia had never seen mild-mannered Sarah so angry. She pulled her knees under her chin and cowered under her covers.

"Did you hear Lucretia leave, Amelia?"

"No, not at all. I was out like a light last night."

"Quick. Hurry up and get dressed. We must find Mr Thomas."

"Hasn't she just gone for a walk?"

"No, look!" bellowed Sarah, yanking back the covers in a fury to reveal the deception.

Amelia smiled at the belongings languishing in the middle of the bed.

'So, she's gone, has she. Good. Life will be a lot easier without her around.'

"Quickly, there's no time to waste! Get up! We must find her!"

"Alright, I'm coming," Amelia groaned.

'But I won't look that hard.'

11

THE REALISATION

"Master Beadle!"

Sarah crashed through the door of Thomas's cottage.

"What on earth is going on?" he grizzled, opening his door, pulling his dressing gown around him.

"What's all the fuss for?" Victor added dozily from the armchair, having spent most of the night in and out of consciousness, comforting Spike.

"It's Lucretia! She's gone, Thomas."

"She's probably just gone for a walk."

"I doubt it."

Sarah explained the deception. Thomas's face stiffened as the words came tumbling out of her mouth.

"Quickly, we must find her. She can't have gone far. Victor, get Spike ready. We must leave now."

Everyone was at full action stations, scurrying round the cottages getting their warm coats and hats on. Within a minute, Spike had been hitched to the cart and Victor, who had slept in his clothes that night, sat poised, waiting for the other three to arrive.

"Gee up, Spike," said Victor.

"Can't you make him go faster?" snared Thomas.

"No, he's had no sleep either because he was stood out in the storm all night. You're lucky he's not run off too. I told you he needed proper stabling."

The cart rumbled out of the yard. Thomas gave everyone their duties.

"Sarah, you look to the left. Amelia, right. I shall look behind. Victor, you keep an eye on the road ahead. You know how treacherous it is."

"Yes," they said in unison.

"She hardly knows anybody in the village. The only English speaker I can think of is Daffyd, so let's try there. Unless she's gone to the station?"

With their eyes peeled, they scanned the landscape, but there was no sign of the girl. Victor wondered what time it was. He fumbled in his pocket, but his watch wasn't at the end of its chain. *'Silly me leaving it at home.'*

"What time do you call this?" said an irate Daffyd as he opened the door.

"It's Lucretia. Is she here?"

"No, of course not. What are you on about, man?"

"Never mind. She's missing. Run off, we think. If you see her, leave a note at the cottage?"

"Ok, Thomas. Best of luck. She'll turn up soon. She's still very much a city girl. She'll come back with her tail between her legs. I'll let Elsie know, and we'll look out for her, I promise."

Down in the ravine, Lucretia heard the cart clutter past, but she was too weak to shout. Her mouth was dry, apart from the bloodied holes where her front teeth had been knocked out in the fall. Her cracked lips were caked with blood. It had been almost a day since she had eaten, and, with several broken bones, she was very frail.

The Greek inscription on the stolen watch had a tragic poignancy to it. If Lucretia could have translated it, no doubt she would have agreed.

"It is better in times of need to have a friend rather than money."

Lucretia was definitely in need of a friend. She wanted to touch the watch to make sure she still had it. It was her insurance policy out of this mess. With a Herculean effort, she managed to get her right hand into her pocket. Glass splinters cut into her fingers, and hot blood soaked into her clammy clothing. Her soul was crushed. The broken watch was worthless. Her left hand dug into the mud, clawing at the bank of the stream. She inched her way out of the icy water, and in tears, she pondered what to do next. The road was nearly twenty feet above her. Unless someone looked down, unless a miracle happened, she had a feeling she was about to meet her maker.

The four desperate searchers hopped back onto the cart. Thomas was beside himself with remorse. If there was one thing that ever got to him, it was a lapse in his ethics. He was supposed to be nurturing the girls, that was the deal, and now one was missing. It was all the more galling as he'd gone to all the trouble of finding a new apprenticeship with the milliner. Not only had he failed Lucretia, but he had failed his friend. *'I hope she turns up before I have to confess the truth. If only he told her last night, she wouldn't be missing.'*

Then his mind returned to the awkward conversation he was going to have with his aunt's milliner, unsure who would be angrier with him, the hatmaker for wasting her time, or his spinster aunt for showing him up.

'How dare she deceived me when I've given her a home. She's going to be for the high jump when I find her,' thought Thomas as his eyes covered every inch of the lane.

Everyone else's minds were blank, focusing every ounce of concentration on looking for the girl. The weather was on the turn again, the harsh Welsh winter in full force. When they reached the end of the lane, there had been no sight of the girl anywhere, and no one working in the fields that morning had seen her either.

Victor pulled up outside the train station, and Thomas leapt off the wagon faster than a greyhound leaving a trap.

He rapped his knuckles on the ticket office window, giving the man on the early shift that day quite a shock. He leapt out of his chair, then repositioned his wonky glasses on his nose.

"Have you sold a lone girl a ticket, possibly to London?" asked Thomas with a note of urgency.

"I haven't seen anyone fitting that description," replied the clerk.

Thomas ran away without even thanking the man for the information. Unaware that the watch had been stolen, he was more concerned with finding the station master, thinking there might have been a kerfuffle if she tried to board a train without a ticket. *'Perhaps she's at the police station?'*

Neither the station master nor any of the porters had helped Lucretia board a train. Her disappearance was becoming increasingly mysterious and worrying. Sarah, in particular, began to suspect that some harm might have come to the girl.

"Let's go back and see if she's returned to the house. Perhaps now the weather's worsened, she's decided she won't run away after all?"

Spike hauled them back to the little cottages as fast as possible, but of course, there was nobody there. It was then that Victor noticed that the watch was missing.

"She's definitely run away, Thomas. That little pocket watch you gave me, it's gone."

For the rest of the day, the women waited at home as Thomas, Victor and Daffyd scouted the landscape on foot and on the cart.

There was no sign.

That night, Thomas felt he had no option but to inform the police that the girl was missing, although he decided not to mention the stolen watch. She'd be in enough trouble when he caught up with her, let alone the law. He repeatedly rehearsed what he was going to say on the long run down to Bala.

"Try not to worry yourself," said Sergeant Llewellyn. "She probably thought she could get a job at one of those hotels in Llandudno or something. She'll be fine. I'll speak to the local constabularies in the area, send a telegram. I'm sure I'll have some good news for you soon. She won't be the first to be tempted by the bright lights of a seaside resort."

Thomas gave a detailed description, and one of the officers made a sketch of her face.

"She's lucky to have a boss like you. Lots of wealthy folk wouldn't care if one of their servants ran away. Two a penny, those people. They can be a feckless bunch when it suits them. Wasn't Irish was she? They have a bit of the devil in 'em."

Thomas gave a weak smile.

"No. Please do what you can to find her."

Despite informing Sergeant Llewellyn, and every constabulary within fifty miles of Bala, no news was forthcoming. A piece in the local newspaper saying a servant had absconded brought no new leads.

Poor old Amelia bore the brunt of Thomas's sole focus. He decided to keep busy as Sergeant Llewellyn's hunt for the missing girl continued. As the days rolled on, the instruction became more arduous.

The relentless curriculum rumbled on, learning reams of Shakespearean sonnets by heart, explaining geometric principles, sketching out how a steam engine worked, as well as recounting endless tales from Greek mythology. How Amelia wished Lucretia had taken her with her.

She regretted their bickering. If she had buried the hatchet with her childhood foe, she too would be free. She guessed the watch was worth several pounds, plenty for both of them to live on as they started their lives again. *'Still, she always was selfish.'*

In between the academic sessions, there was the daily walk to the police station for news of Lucretia—in a week, there had been no sightings of her. There was instruction in agriculture, tending to a new kitchen garden that had taken Amelia an age to dig over. Thomas offered no help at all, saying the physical exertion was good for her constitution, and the vegetables would be good for her too. With what little strength she had left, she helped Sarah with household chores. After that, she mucked out the corner where Spike stood, under a simple wooden roof she had built with Victor.

Sarah stared out of the window, her face frosty with concern.

"He's working that girl too hard," said Sarah as
she saw Amelia weeding the new vegetable patch.
"She'll run off to London or wherever like
Lucretia. You mark my words."

"I hope not," said Victor, not just because
Lucretia's disappearance was becoming a concern
the longer it ran on, but because secretly, the
pretty girl battling outside was stealing his heart.

The longer they spent together, it was obvious the experiment between her and Thomas would never lead to anything more than some sort of practical arrangement. If they were to marry, there would never be any affection, and he felt Amelia deserved better. On the few occasions he'd been alone with the girl like when they built Spike's shelter, he'd found her charming company and felt a wonderful butterfly feeling in his heart every time she looked at him.

"Don't you be getting sweet on her now," said
Sarah. "She belongs to Master Thomas until this
experiment of his is over."

Victor admitted nothing, hiding the awkward silence by throwing some more logs on the fire.

Thomas, however, had no intention of easing up on the training. In fact, he decided he was going to make it more difficult, especially now there was more riding on the one woman left.

He announced the next phase of the girl's training after their evening meal. Amelia wasn't party to the discussions. She had gone to flop into bed the minute her plate was clear.

"Victor, Sarah. I'm going to see how Amelia copes on a camping trip. We shall go tomorrow for one night. Then I suggest you pack up this place, and we will return to the hall in Abingdon. It's clear Lucretia has settled somewhere else. There's no point staying here rubbing salt into the wounds."

"Right you are, Mr Thomas," said the two aides in unison.

"We'll get everything packed up and ready," said Sarah. "We travelled light, so it won't take long."

"I'll send a telegram to the shopkeeper and arrange for a delivery of some basics to be sent to us when we arrive in Abingdon," added Victor. "I can do it when I go to the police station. I presume you won't have time if you're off into the hills?"

"Excellent, Victor," I can always rely on you.

"I'll go first thing. Right, that's me done. I can barely keep my eyes open."

Sarah nodded with a yawn as they made their way to their beds, with Victor discussing the finer arrangements for the morning.

Thomas made some excuses, saying he was going to enjoy a good slug of brandy in front of the fire. Twenty minutes later, he checked they were asleep and was delighted to see that they were. It gave him time to polish his favourite hunting pistol and get it ready for the hike. He checked there were at least two bullets in its six chambers. *'Wonderful'.*

12

THE DISCOVERY

"Amelia," yelled Thomas.

"I'm just out here feeding the geese their breakfast before we head off. I thought you would want me to do that. You normally do." she replied defensively.

"Well, you can stop doing that. It's time to go. We're going to see where the harpist fled when the lake was flooded. Would you like that?"

"Alright," came the timid reply.

Amelia had learned to say she would be delighted to do whatever Thomas suggested. It made things easier, if not more palatable.

'What sort of a word is alright?' muttered Thomas to himself. *'What is the point of me teaching her the works of the greatest English writers for her to resort to slang. I will be glad when this education phase is over.'*

"Pass me my bag, will you?" asked Thomas.

Amelia grabbed the knapsack and groaned.

"What's in here? it weighs a ton!"

"Never you mind. Just pass it over."

"It's going to be bitterly cold up there," she complained.

"And that's exactly why I have taught you how to gather kindling and build a fire in the bothy. It's another learning opportunity."

"What's a bothy again? Remember, I am a Londoner, Master Thomas."

"It's a shepherd's hut. Please don't tell me you have forgotten what a shepherd is!" he snapped, not waiting for an answer. "Come on now, we're heading back to Oxfordshire tomorrow. We haven't got all day."

Victor watched the poor girl try and keep up with Thomas. He was wearing hunting gear, much better suited to the extreme weather. Amelia was still in her milking maid dress with a shawl. Quickly, he grabbed his oilskin jacket and ran up the hill to give it to her.

"Here, take this. It's mine, but I won't need it just going to the village and back."

"Good thinking, Victor. I should have organised that earlier. I am all over the place today. Can't seem to focus on anything."

Victor shot back to Sarah and gave her a hand with the packing.

"I don't think we should leave before we find Lucretia," Sarah warned as she washed the breakfast plates and Victor dried them. "It feels like we've abandoned the girl. Sir Richard is going to go ballistic when he finds out."

"Yes, but who will tell him? We won't."

"Daniel, silly."

"Ah yes. He's been wary of Thomas's motivation from the start, really. I don't think that book's been a good influence on Thomas. He's been riddled with melancholia since he discovered it. "

As the two lone hikers yomped up the hill, Thomas's mind was set on engineering the hardest task yet for Amelia, where she would know what it felt like to fight for her life.

'I wish Lucretia was still here,' lamented Amelia five paces behind Thomas. *'I'm getting all the hardship and none of the benefits. Now that I'm the only one left. I bet she's having the time of her life at Llandudno or wherever she's ended up. There are certainly going to be no benefits staying at a tumbled down bothy even the hardy shepherds avoid."*

"Crikey, look at the time, Victor. You better get into the village."

"Jeepers!" he said, "flying out of the door."

"Victor, what about your coat?"

He waved his hand dismissively and went to fetch the cart. Spike was in a good mood, nuzzling his nose against Victor's hand as they got ready for the off. The horse had hoped it had a sugar lump in it. He was in luck.

"So, you found it then," he giggled. "There you go, boy, you tuck into that. And have another."

The two of them did their trek into Bala. Victor hummed a tune to pass the time, gleeful that the time in Wales would soon be over. Spike plodded on obediently, like a donkey at Blackpool. The scenery might be stunning, but life in the cottages was hard, the regular slog to the village being a case in point. No errand boy would ever make the journey up the hill, so he was left to get provisions. "'Two more trips, then that's it, Spikey, boy."

He slumped into a trance, watching the horse's muscular shoulders rise and fall as he walked, he made a mental note of what they would need in Abingdon.

He was shocked out of his daydream. Spike flinched, and the cart lurched awkwardly down the hill. A young game-keeper's son ran up from the slippery ravine, right in front of the cart. It took all of Victor's skill to bring everything to a rapid halt.

"Watch out," he yelled, relieved he'd not run the lad over.

Victor went to crack Spike's reins, but there was something about the boy's expression that spooked him.

"Dwi wedi dod o hyd i ferch farw wrth y nant. Rhaid inni fynd at yr heddlu!"

Victor had no idea what he was saying. The young lad looked terrified as he beckoned him towards the kerb.

"Calm down, lad. I haven't got a clue what you mean. I bet you want a free ride into town, you lazy little ragamuffin. Or you're going to try and rob me. Well, I've got no money, so you can forget it."

"Rhingyll Llewellyn! "

The second word was familiar, but still, Victor was bemused about what the boy meant. The lad tugged at Victor's sleeve, then pointed to a lump near the ravine's stream. The two of them struggled down the muddy bank, using the protruding rocks as a treacherous staircase.

The boy froze and began to sob. Victor peered down. *'A body! In a milking maid's outfit and an oilskin.'* Victor suddenly understood where he had to go—the police station to see Sergeant Llewellyn.

In a panic, they scrambled up the stones, both looking at each other, praying neither of them fell. Victor flopped on the top of the road like a seal, relieved to be off the deadly slope. He grabbed the lad's hand and pulled him up to safety and onto the wagon.

"Don't want you tumbling down there, do we?" he said with a smile.

The terrified lad held onto the cart, his hands trembling with fear or a lack of stamina or both.

"Come on, Spike, faster!" he yelled as the cart hurtled downhill faster than The Mallard heading for York.

All Victor could think was, *'Is it her?'*

13

THE FINAL STRAW

"Why's the landscape so ugly up here, Thomas?" yelled Amelia into the wind. "It's all grey. Dead looking."

"It's not ugly. It is a wonder. The scars are where the earth yielded its beautiful Welsh slate. Renowned worldwide as the best roofing material known to man."

Amelia still thought the splintered slag heaps as far as the eye could see were not a celebration of commerce but hideous. Like the land had caught smallpox. She was glad when they rounded the hill and onto a much prettier, unspoilt area. Up on an exposed ledge was the bothy. It looked far more welcoming from a distance than it did up close.

"Have you got some food in the bag, Thomas? I'm starving."

"No," he said grumpily. "We'll be setting snares to catch our own food later. I've made some ready to deploy."

Amelia didn't like the idea of finding a bunny rabbit squirming on the ground, trapped, half-strangulated, as

Thomas yelled at her to cave its head in with a stone. One more lecture about the self-sufficiency of Spartan women or ancient African tribes, and she would explode. *'Life might have been dull at the mission, but at least you knew what was happening next.'*

The small dry-stone building was draughty and cold. The wind whistled through the gaps between the slabs of stone, and the loose metal sheeting fluttered against the joists when the breeze picked up.

"Here, this will warm you up."

She took a seat on a raised stone platform, part-bed, part-bench. Thomas handed her one of two hip flasks. She took a swig and choked on the strong liquor. It was her first taste of spirits, and she understood why it was called 'fire-water' in an instant.

"Light some of these. I'll push some mud in the gaps. Make it a bit nicer in here."

He handed her two big white candles, the sort that would normally adorn a high altar in a cathedral, and a box of Bryant and May, with five matches inside. As soon as she struck the first one, it was blown out. The second suffered the same fate. She didn't want to waste any more and waited for Thomas to return.

Thomas was gone for what seemed like an age. She only knew he was nearby when she saw the flickering light near a hole as he worked to fill it with moss, mud or whatever else came to hand.

With the gaps plugged, the bothy began to be a little more homely. She risked one more candle, shielding the feeble little flame with the hand. *'At last!'* The little orange flame leapt from the thin wood across to the fat black candle wick, and it began to burn brightly. The warm light cheered her soul, and the size of them told her they would last the night. She pushed the other candle up towards its twin and smiled as the light flooded the little shelter. The creamy white wax liquefied, and the light grew brighter still. She looked in the bag for some kindling and small logs. *'He's always so organised. Packing them on the top, ready to use.'* As her eyes adjusted to the lighting, she saw a small hearth, and that was where she lit the small fire. She tried a little bit more of the hip flask. It made her head spin and her belly feel homely.

In the warmth, it was inevitable that tipsy Amelia began to doze, exhausted from the yomp, the lessons, the lectures, and the backbreaking work she'd been tasked with from dawn to dusk ever since she was out of her sickbed.

With all the holes plugged, Thomas returned to the bothy and closed the rickety door. He stared into the flames, possessed by them. His head tilted back as he drained the last drops of drink from his flask. Still craving more liquor, he gently slid the other tin from Amelia's fingers and quaffed that too. Amelia, like one of Jimmy McGinty's bare-knuckle fighters, was out for the count.

Thomas watched the little puddle of wax grow deeper. Soon there was almost a tablespoonful pooling around each wick.

His knapsack toppled over, and some of the things fell out with a clunk. Amelia gave a groan. He pushed the hunting pistol back into the bag, pulled out a handkerchief, and quickly closed the buckle. As the quiet returned, Amelia began to snore lightly.

Thomas prodded her cheek with his finger. There was no response. He whipped out the handkerchief, rolled it up quickly and then flattened it into a blindfold.

"Amelia," he whispered, but there was no response.

He whipped the fabric around her eyes, blindfolding her.

Then it was a waiting game until she came round a little bit. He ferreted about in the bag and pulled out the pistol, then stared into the candle. He was ready. Outside, night began to fall.

*

Amelia's eyelashes scratched against the fabric, startling her.

"What's going on? Thomas? Are you there?" she whispered as her hands reached up towards the blindfold.

"Yes. Leave that where it is. It's time for another little challenge to test how resilient you are. Sit still."

Nodding as he grabbed her arm, he slid her sleeve up to her elbow, exposing the flat side of her slender forearm, and began the test.

"Now, whatever I do next, I don't want you to flinch."

Just the words made her want to panic, but thanks to Thomas's borderline cruelty, she could hide the feeling perfectly. She took her mind to a happier place, and after a deep, slow breath, in and out, she waited. Then he did as he said. Her head shot back in shock, banging against the rocky interior of the bothy.

"I told you not to flinch," he tutted as he put down one of the candles and picked up the other one, needing more liquid wax to drip on her.

She tried to reach across and touch her arm, desperate to identify what was causing the horrible burning sensation. It stung, but not like when she had scalded herself once with some hot water or collided with some nettles by mistake.

"What are you doing?" asked the girl.

Thomas pinned her in place and prepared to drip more wax on her arm. She squirmed, desperate to pull away. Vulnerable and alone with a man who was becoming more of a monster by the minute, she squealed in horror.

He lifted the candle, positioning it carefully. The hot wax dripped onto her arm, forming little rivers that solidified in seconds. She yelped in pain.

"Be silent, or I will make you pay," he warned, the smell of stale alcohol filling her nose.

Amelia became fearful. Thomas had always been a little cruel, but now he was sinking into barbarism.

"Not a word. Sit still," he hissed.

He let the wax form again as he pinned poor Amelia's body against the wall. Still weakened from the disease, her poor appetite and poor sleep, there was no way she could wrestle him off. She did everything in her power to stay motionless. She tilted her head slightly and peered through the tiniest of slits at the bottom of the blindfold. Relieved, it was just enough of a view to see Thomas lean in with the candle again. As he raised his arm, she bit the inside of her cheek and stiffened her whole body. When the dripping wax hit her soft skin this time, it was like Thomas had dropped it on a marble statue she was that still.

"Betterrrr," slurred Thomas.

'Once this is over, I shall run away like Lucretia.'

Dazed and frightened, she heard Thomas block the exit with a small wooden object, probably one of the old chairs. He returned to her and pulled at her skirt. She was terrified he would pull it up to her waist, but he seemed to give up on the idea.

'What's he doing?'

His breathing was heavy and laboured. Her head began to throb with pain as the brandy wore off. Sensing impending peril, she needed all her faculties, and she regretted having a single sip. She peered through the chink in the blindfold and saw him reaching in the knapsack again. Then there was the unmistakable glint from the silvery gun barrel and the sound of it being prepped to fire.

Thomas double-checked the number of bullets. *'Two just as I planned.'*

With a gasp, Amelia's eyes open wide, the lashes snagging against the blindfold again. The metal glinted from the candlelight as he made his final checks. *'That's it. He's finally lost it. He's going to kill me and then himself. Surely? His beloved experiment has failed.'*

She was absolutely terrified, but she didn't dare scream, wanting to cling to the last few seconds of life. The blood was banging in her ears, and she was sure he could hear her heart banging in her chest.

"What are you going to do, Thomas?" she asked, but there was no response.

She tried to count the seconds mentally in her head to measure the passage of time. Was it hurtling by or crawling? It was hard to tell. She was too afraid to concentrate and kept having to start again. One thing was for certain, Thomas was toying with her and was not going to give any clue as to when her life would be over. There was a metallic clicking sound.

'Is this it?'

Her breath was stuck in her throat. She didn't make even the faintest of movements in case it provoked Thomas further. And then there was the second click as the trigger was pulled, followed by the loudest bang Amelia had ever heard in her life. And yet, there was no pain. Her ears rang out. She jumped a foot in the air before landing back down on the stone bench.

"Stop flinching," yelled Thomas, as the smell of burning fabric filled her nostrils.

He had shot at through her clothing, though she had no idea if that was a mistake or deliberate, wondering if the liquor had made him miss the target.

There was another one of the faint clicks again as the gun was primed once more. Her survival instinct made her flinch again, desperate for her to fight her way through the door and onto safety. There was another almighty bang, then silence. Thomas had shot the bullet through the metal roof. That was it for Amelia. The adrenaline gave her the energy she needed to overpower the increasingly drunken Thomas. She pushed him back over the table, and he lost his footing. Tossing the chair to one side, she flung the door open and ran out into the black night, wanting to be somewhere, anywhere, but there in the bothy. She ran down the path towards the cottages.

The cold air hit Thomas and sharpened his senses, quickly sobering him up enough to go in pursuit, but she was too nimble for him, and soon there was no way he would catch her. Alone, walking back through the scarred slate works, he regretted his actions. Things had gotten very much out of hand. *'She will always lack a backbone,'* he lamented.

All Amelia could think of was the yellow lights of the cottages in the distance. The clouds had cleared, and the moonlit sky guided her way. Goodness knows how she would have coped if it had been a foggy night. She burst into the cottage like a dervish, giving Victor and Sarah quite a fright. They had been discussing poor Lucretia's demise ever since Llewellyn's men had identified the decomposing body that afternoon. She ran to them.

"What on earth's happened to you, my poor girl? Where's Thomas?"

"I don't know, and I don't care," she sobbed as she clung onto Sarah with all her might.

Sarah looked at Victor. Both of them knew what they needed to do, and that was protect the girl from Thomas. Enough was enough. The poor girl was an absolute wreck, unable to speak, despite Sarah giving her the third degree to discover what had happened. The red burn marks on her arm were a concern, as was the scorched round hole in her skirt. When Sarah said to Victor that she thought she saw a shadowy figure approaching the cottages, Amelia became hysterical, and she shrieked, in snatched syllables:

"Keep—him—a—way—from—me!"

Now wasn't the time to tell her about Lucretia's demise, but it would soon become common knowledge in the little cottage's front room. The wooden door crashed into the plaster, as Thomas announced:

"There you are."

He marched towards Amelia. Victor darted in between them, and the two men began to wrestle, as Amelia screamed:

"He's got a gun, be careful, Victor."

It would be Sarah who put an end to the fracas.

"Stop it, Thomas. This has gone on long enough. Lucretia might be dead. I will not let you take the life of another girl because of your stupid standards."

The news of the body in the ditch finally brought the maudlin figure of Thomas Beadle to his senses. He poured another large brandy, then went to his bedroom, slamming the door behind him. He pondered his next move. Victor and Sarah did their best to calm Amelia down.

'She'll have to go. I would have been better off trying to find a society wife and knocking the airs and graces out of her,' he fumed as he stared at the ceiling.

Later that night, there was a knock at the door. It was Sergeant Llewellyn. He broke the sad news that a search of the body had shown it matched Lucretia's description.

"Get Mr Thomas and Amelia now, Sarah," said Victor.

"Tea, sergeant?"

He nodded.

"Two sugars if you have them. And milk. I need to keep my strength up on a day like today."

The tea sloshed into the cup and gave off a plume of hot steam until the milk was added. Llewellyn cupped his hands around it before fumbling in his pocket. The trio stared at an envelope he retrieved. The officer passed to Victor.

"We'll need a formal identification, of course. But I must warn you, she's not in a good way. So perhaps you could confirm this belongs to one of you."

Victor lifted the flap and peered inside. The sight of the bloodied watch greeted him. He didn't need to turn it over to read the inscription. He knew in his gut it was his. Thomas snatched the little paper wallet and saw the familiar engraving. Victor spoke up.

"This is mine, sergeant. She stole it the morning she left. It's definitely Lucretia. I recognised the jacket as one of Mr Thomas's, but I didn't say anything. I was hoping this awful news wasn't true."

"Well, the coroners had an initial look at her, and he thinks it was an accident. There is no question of foul play. Looks like she tripped and fell. Her hands were scratched and bruised from trying to protect herself during the fall."

The trio hanging on the officer's every word all gave a sigh of relief.

"Although, judging by the pattern of the bleeding, death wasn't instant."

They stared at the blood on the cracked watch face and gulped in horror.

"We were planning to go back to Abingdon tomorrow," said Amelia. "Can we? Or do you need us here?"

Thomas kicked her leg under the table, furious she was thinking of herself after such sad news. All Amelia could think of was running away herself, and, after poor Lucretia's experience, that would be a lot easier in Oxfordshire than the barren mountains of Snowdonia.

"Good question. No, that's fine. Just formalities here now. We can send the body on the train for you to organise the funeral in a day or two."

Sergeant Llewellyn made his excuses and left, promising to keep them updated.

"Well, that's that, then," said Thomas, in a morose voice, before returning to his room.

Amelia was petrified. She delved into Thomas's knapsack and took the pistol out of it, and gave it to Victor for safekeeping. At first, she played with the handkerchief that had been her blindfold, rolling it over and over between her fingers, not wanting to say a word about her ordeal in the bothy. Feeling their eyes bore into her, the confession tumbled out. Open-mouthed, Sarah and Victor listened as the girl explained how she came to know the gun was in the knapsack and the awful night she'd had with Thomas.

"Don't worry, my girl," Victor comforted. "We're going to tell Thomas that this experiment ends right now before we lose another girl."

"But he doesn't listen to anyone. Logic drives him, warped logic granted, but in his mind, this is all acceptable."

"He'll listen to his Aunt Mimi."

"When she says what, exactly, Victor?" asked Sarah.

"When she says she needs a live-in maid."

Sarah looked unconvinced.

"Mimi always needs staff. She is such a miserable harpy they never stay long. It will give Thomas an opportunity to get rid of you without losing face. Then perhaps, you will be free of the torture."

It didn't really sound like it to Amelia. It had all the hallmarks of jumping out of the frying pan into the fire, but she thanked Victor anyway.

"Perfect," she said with a perfectly rehearsed fake smile normally reserved for Thomas. "Well, I'd better turn in. We have a busy day tomorrow."

They all retired and had a sleepless night imagining poor Lucretia's last hours alone in the ravine. Life couldn't get any worse for any of them. They all felt guilty, thinking they could and should have done more. Finally, the motley crew had crashed to rock bottom. And it was all Thomas's fault and his wretched philosophical zeal.

"He got Amelia into this mess, and he is going to get her out of it," whispered Sarah sensing Victor tossing and turning in his bed.

Next door, Amelia, feeling like a snared rabbit herself faced with the Hobson's choice of life with Thomas or that harridan Aunt Mimi, cried herself to sleep.

On the long journey back, Sarah and Victor outwardly convinced Thomas that Aunt Mimi was the answer. Inside, he thought boarding school was a better option but had no means to fund it, with all his assets tied up in the hall until his trust fund was released by the courts—and that was two years.

14

MIMI'S SOIRÉE

As Amelia tried to lock the door to her squalid basement room, she knew that life with Great Aunt Mimi was definitely worse than struggling with Thomas. At least with Thomas, her academic and practical education had been beneficial, sometimes even entertaining. She had enjoyed Victor and Sarah's company. Alas, there were no such moments of levity in Mimi's household.

The old spinster had a three-story townhouse on a posh Georgian square in Oxford, where she lived with two equally dour servants, Mr and Mrs Harper, who helped keep the house running smoothly.

It was hard to decide who was the most callous of the three of them. Amelia was amazed that Sarah and Victor had thought life would be easier there than with Thomas, but she supposed, at least they wouldn't get drunk and threaten her with a pistol. Although she could afford more servants, like Thomas, she preferred 'frugality and necessity;' to 'needless expense'. Each morning, the basement door would be unlocked at 5am sharp. It felt such an ungodly hour with so little sleep.

"If you are to thrive, you are up at five," Mrs Harper had warned one morning when Amelia hid her head under the bedcovers, hoping it was all a nightmare she could wake up from. The harridan arrived as regular as clockwork and gave Amelia her tasks for the day. There was never a second for the poor girl to herself. It was wall-to-wall drudgery from the moment she awoke to the time her tired head flopped on the pillow at night. With only three staff, Amelia was expected to muck in and do a range of tasks, be they formal duties or chores. Mrs Harper had been quick to lay the law down.

"As a 'maid-of-all work', your responsibilities include lighting fires, sweeping the floors and hearths, cleaning the grates, dishwashing, washing the marble fireplaces, dusting and polishing chairs, tables and other furniture, shaking out rugs and curtains, dusting window frames, ledges and doors, dusting ornaments, glasses and china, preparing and cooking meals, making the beds and laundry."

"Yes, Mrs Harper."

"You will get up before Miss Beadle, make sure the main rooms are warm, make breakfast, and then start the chores that will keep you busy for the rest of the day. We have set days, such as wash day and dusting day, where you will be given additional duties. Oh, and before I forget, once a week, Miss Beadle will take a bath. She will expect you to run buckets of hot water upstairs for a bath for her."

"Yes, Mrs Harper. Once a week. Got that."

The old woman picked up a massive, galvanised bucket and filled it with water.

"Thirty of these is usually enough."

Mimi Beadle, like Thomas, rejected the finer things in life, but she drew the line at cold bathwater. On picking up the heavy pail, Amelia felt her shoulder bones almost pull apart with the strain. *'Thirty!'*

Her first days were filled with the endless blacking of hearths and grates, then the dusting of the tops of all cupboards and picture frames for fear of Mimi or Mrs Harper running a disapproving finger along the top of them. As soon as she felt she was making a little headway, Mrs Harper would come with even more work. This treatment lasted for months, with only a half-day on Sunday to provide respite from the monotony. Thomas had awoken an inquisitive side to her, which no longer had an outlet. She quickly lost hope that life would be any better.

This drab existence had gone on for months. It felt like she was doing the lion's share of the hard graft, whilst Mr and Mrs Harper did the easier, more pleasurable tasks like dealing with paperwork or preparing a light lunch. Feeling abandoned, Amelia heard nothing from Beadle. Not a word. Neither Victor nor Sarah had sent so much as a calling card or invited her for tea on Sunday. It would be almost a year later before she learned of her first chance of a visit from Thomas.

She didn't discover the details from him, of course. He wasn't one for letters or calling cards, and the only talking he enjoyed was debating. He was clear he still avoided polite society and normal conversation over tea and cake with the same vigour as the guilty pickpocket in a crowd avoiding the police. It was when she was waiting for the copper to heat up the water for Miss Beadle's weekly bath, she accidentally overheard Mrs Harper discussing it with her husband.

> "Yes, next Saturday night. Master Thomas will be visiting, along with two of his dearest friends. Let us deal with all the formalities. I doubt Thomas will want to see that girl ever again."

Amelia's jaw clamped tightly shut, and she snorted like a bull about to charge. *'He might.'* At first, Amelia hoped the other two guests might be Victor and Sarah, then dismissed the idea. 'Mimi's such a stuffy old bat who would never have someone of their social standing over her threshold unless they were coming in via the servants' entrance to skivvy for her. *'No, it must be someone else. No doubt Daniel is one person. But the other?'* Despite wracking her brains, the second likely guest remained a mystery.

> "Stop daydreaming, Miss Sinden, and get on with your work!" chided Mrs Harper.

Amelia let her frustration be known by clanking around, knocking the heavy bucket against the door frame.

"Careful. You'll have the paint off there, and putting it right will come out of your allowance," nagged Mr Harper.

Angry that nobody thought to tell her that her former master was visiting, she felt more alone than ever. Much as she'd hated how things had ended in Wales, she was interested in finding out how Thomas was faring. Compared to the chaotic tutelage of Mr Beadle, the endless unappreciated drudgery of 25 Beaumont Terrace was a step down, not up.

The list of Amelia's jobs was particularly long prior to Mr Beadle's visit. Several times she felt her eyes droop closed as she had her head down, scrubbing the hearths. She snapped her neck up sharply and blinked a lot, trying to stave off sleep. Thankfully, she managed to hide her exhaustion. Clearly, Mimi wanted to show that the house was kept ship-shape, and she ruled the roost.

On the day of the visit, with the regular chores done to Mimi's and the Harper's exacting standards, Amelia spent most of the morning peeling vegetables, then making pastry before a final stint of dusting the front parlour and dining room. It was ten to seven by the time she had finished.

"You can go now, Amelia. You are dismissed," ordered Mimi.

Dutifully the girl sped down the backstairs and sat in her room. For once, Mr and Mrs Harper slipped up. With all the other duties, they had and forgot to lock Amelia in her room, but she was too tired to notice. She had dozed the minute she got in her room, and she assumed it was locked.

There was a clang of the doorbell and some loud voices as the guests were welcomed. Drowsily, she listened in. *'Who could the others be?'* She tried a process of elimination. With Thomas such an oddball, she didn't think it would take long. He'd become such a loner in Wales, his list of friends was even shorter. He didn't even mention Daniel during their time there. *'Perhaps they're from that posh society of his, those thinkers from the university.'*

"Do come in," said Mr Harper, showing Thomas and his companions to the parlour. "Miss Beadle, your guests are here." The floorboards creaked as the footsteps paced across the hallway. Down in the dank basement, looking at the exact spot on the grubby ceiling where the sounds came from didn't help Amelia solve the question of *'who are the other two.'*

"Well, this is a surprise, Daniel and Richard. How wonderful to see you!"

Daniel and Thomas's friendship had quickly rekindled as Daniel helped his cash-strapped friend pass his bar exams. Sir Richard, now an MP, had spent a lot of time at his Shrewsbury constituency, and it was the first time that Richard had seen Thomas in quite some time. In his rush to get elected, he had not kept tabs on what Thomas had done at the mission. They had exchanged terse correspondence when Sir Richard read about Lucretia's death in the newspaper saying she was the former servant of his household, and he *demanded to know what the blazes were going on.'* Despite the death being proven as accidental by the coroner, Wentworth was livid. Things had been strained ever since Richard had discovered Thomas's ruse to use his name as a front for his acquisition of the girls, and he was waiting for the truth to come out. So far, he and Thomas had dodged that bullet.

Before going to Mimi's, Daniel had suggested a few drinks at the Victoria Arms, overlooking the Cherwell, but Richard and Thomas argued about Cromwell after seeing a notice on the wall that the former Lord Protector had visited the watering hole back in the day.

"Good old Oliver letting his hair down for once. Cheers!" chirped Richard, then licked his lips before tackling the glorious ale.

"He didn't drink here, Richard, you buffoon. He used the ferry. This was the ferryman's cottage."

"For goodness' sake, lighten up, Thomas. It was a joke. Everyone knows Oliver was bald," Wentworth joked, infuriating Thomas more.

"No, he wasn't. My grandfather said he saw Cromwell's embalmed head on display at Mead Court, Bond Street, in James Cox's Curiosity shop. Said he had a full head of hair."

"Stop it, you two!" snipped Daniel Astley, putting his hand between the two men's faces like a referee at a bare-knuckle fight. "We are supposed to be enjoying ourselves."

"That's unlikely with a night at Great Aunt Mimi's ahead of us," moaned Thomas.

"I know you're dreading it, but if she won't report back on how Amelia is faring, then we'll have to do our own digging, won't we?"

"Yes! Reverend Bennett's been on my back asking about the girls—girl. I keep making excuses. He is going to find out we deceived him, then we'll all be for the high jump. You mark my words. I was lucky that Bala is on the coaching route from Shrewsbury to Llandudno."

"Drink up, time to go," said a tipsy Daniel Astley, who had two drinks to the other men's one because he had kept quiet and not got drawn into their petty arguments.

"Do come through," said Mr Harper, bowing and scraping.

Sir Wentworth was probably the highest-ranking person he'd ever met.

"Go and bring the first course, please, Harper," said Miss Beadle. "I am sure you strapping fellows are starving. How does potato soup sound, freshly made today?"

All three nodded, muttering how delightful it sounded, even though their stomachs were still full of ale.

Mrs Harper dished out the first course, served with reverence from Mimi's best Sèvres porcelain tureen. She winced as Harper clumsily banged the lid against one of the 24-carat gold plated handles before he took it away, giving him her icy *'careful'* stare.

"This smells wonderful, Great Aunt Mimi," said Thomas.

Daniel disagreed, thinking it smelt of nothing at all, not even potato.

Back in the scullery, Mrs and Mrs Harper dashed about preparing the main course. They really needed Amelia's help, but their spite drove them to make sure she was kept well away from the guests. Mimi had made it clear it was alright to see and hear some servants that night, but not her, fearing encountering her might trigger Thomas's melancholia again.

As the silver soup spoons politely tapped the bowls as they ate, not a word was uttered, the ambience frosty felt by all. Mimi, like Thomas, was the sort of sour-faced person who would enter a busy room, and it would feel as if ten happy people had left. She was always bristling. Daniel couldn't help but think that Thomas had got some of his solitary traits from her. Often, his parents bundled young Thomas off to stay with her for the summer holidays, so they could travel on the continent unimpeded by the youth's awkward presence.

During the summer holidays at Oxford, the two youths would hire a boat near Magdalen College, punt down the river, and chew the fat of life. Daniel thought back to Thomas telling him about his time at boarding school, which led him to a convenient segue to mention Amelia, who, so far, had been the elephant in the room.

"So, how is Amelia doing at boarding school, Thomas?"

"Yes, do tell me," said Richard.

Mr Harper nearly dropped the silver platter of roast beef he was carrying when he heard the news. *'She's certainly not at boarding school, in front of an ironing or washboard, more like.'* grinned the horrible man. He hated seeing anyone enjoy themselves, apart from Mimi, and she seldom enjoyed anything, on principle.

"Actually, I meant to tell you about that, Daniel," said Thomas after an awkward cough. "Mimi here has taken her on as a housemaid. She gets to stay in the Oxford area near Victor and Sarah. And she's learning a lot on the job."

"She is?" asked Daniel.

"Yes, you have to admit she wasn't cut out to be an academic or my wife for that matter, but she seems to fit in here."

Daniel couldn't understand how anyone as vivacious as Amelia could fit into Mimi's hellish household. Her existing household staff only liked working there because they were all as miserable as each other. *'A fun-loving girl like*

Amelia would not fit in at all. She thrives on praise, and I bet she gets none of that here.'

"Is that what you told Daniel, Thomas? You lied about boarding school? I cannot believe you sometimes. Why do you always have to lie?"

Thomas said nothing in his defence and instead reached for another slice of beef. He might be his oldest friend, but Daniel wanted to throttle him, providing Sir Richard didn't get to him first. *'She's still alive, I suppose,'* muttered the politician. The last thing he wanted was any sort of scandal. If it came to light in the papers, Amelia was not working at his manor house in Shrewsbury, it would not look good. Investigative journalism was on the rise, and less scrupulous hacks like the exploit of the upper classes were written about mercilessly if it sold more papers.

The meal continued in the same frosty atmosphere. Great Aunt Mimi disliked people at the best of times. Thomas railed against the mores of polite society and loathed small talk. Daniel and Richard were too angry to enter into chit-chat, even when their bellies were full of food and wine. Misery reigned supreme, despite Mr Harper bringing up his wife's jaw-droppingly good bread and butter pudding, doused with lashings of an all-new magical product, Bird's Custard, which was the talk of dinner tables up and down the land.

Mrs Harper went downstairs to give Amelia her last job of the day. She went to turn the key in the lock and found the door already open. *'Arthur! Why do even the most basic of tasks get overlooked? I swear I have to do everything myself if I want it done right.'*

"Amelia, wake up, you feckless girl! Can you light the fires in all the guest rooms, please? Miss Beadle's visitors will be retiring soon," she bellowed, shaking the girl by her shoulders, then stomping back up the stairs to reprimand Arthur before Amelia had even replied.

"Where have you been?" snapped Arthur.

"Downstairs. How many more times do I have to tell you? Every time we leave her on her own, we must lock the door. She cannot be trusted. If she runs away then, goodness knows what Mimi will say."

The beleaguered husband gave the nod. His wife was right yet again, and he made sure he told her as much.

Amelia gathered some coals from the scuttle in the back yard, then took the servant stairs to the smallest of the three guestrooms. There was no opportunity to peer around the dining room door to spy on who was there. She presumed that Thomas would be in the largest bed-room, but she had no idea who the other two might be destined for.

She knelt down and held a long household match beside one of the firelighters. It was stubborn to light, or perhaps she was not watching what she was doing. The dancing flame and the blackness creeping up the wooden match-stick reminded her of being back in the bothy and lighting the candles for Thomas. Then there was the memory of him delighting in dropping the molten wax on her. She shuddered, then she leapt out of her skin as the bedroom door opened.

Daniel Astley had tired of the acidic atmosphere in the parlour, and not even a large quantity of custard or a large sherry could dull the unpleasantness of it. He'd excused himself and dashed up to his room before the below-stairs jungle drums could announce his departure. He wasn't expecting to see Amelia, but he was delighted when he did.

"It's you!" he blurted out as he looked at the girl in front of him. Scanning her figure by eye, more as a friend than a lothario, he noted she'd lost a lot of weight. All her womanly curves had gone. Only a bony frame remained. *'And she's lost her sparkle.'* The boisterous, flippant girl he had taken to Abingdon with Thomas was gone.

"Daniel, it's good to see you," she said politely, her body not sure if she should curtsey, run away, or give him a desperate hug.

Astley smiled, fearing hugging her would be frowned upon. After all, he was alone with a seventeen-year-old girl in his bedroom.

"I'll, er, leave you to it," he said dismissively, heading off towards the bathroom, sure that if Mrs Harper found them, there would be hell to pay for poor Amelia.

He longed to strike up a proper conversation but couldn't. His departure cut through Amelia's heart like a knife. She yanked the bucket of coal off the floor and finished lighting the other two fires. Downbeat, she crept downstairs. Outside her door, Mrs Harper was tapping her toe on the floor, priming herself to box the poor girl's ears for being slow. The harridan stopped when a man's voice called out.

"I think Miss Beadle wants you, Mrs Harper. She said it was urgent."

Keen to look after her mistress promptly, Mrs Harper locked the door, then flew up the stairs.

Desperate to talk to Daniel, or anyone, about her harsh treatment but thwarted, feeling invisible, vulnerable, and unloved, Amelia lay on her bed and sobbed. Her eyes were buried deep in the crook of her elbow, and her mouth butted up against the pillow to stifle the pitiful cries.

Daniel crept down the stairs, silent as a fox, then pushed against a tatty-looking, ill-fitting door. It stayed firmly closed. He grabbed the handle and gave it a good twist. It wouldn't budge. *'Who's that? It can't be the Harpers! Can it?'* she thought as she raised her head slightly. Daniel's hand skimmed the door. At last, his fingers met with a small black key, and he turned it.

Something banged into the door as it opened. Amelia was petrified. *"What if Mrs Harper has come back to beat me with a poker for being insolent?"*

The tears of despair that had run down her face now became tears of joy. At the entrance was Daniel, carrying a tray of leftover cheese, biscuits, and several pats of rich, creamy butter. It looked delightful. Although she got bed and board with Great Aunt Mimi, Mrs Harper kept the rations deliberately meagre, and the standard of food was always going to be below par compared with the meals she made for Mimi.

Saliva flooded into her mouth at the sight of all the treats in front of her.

"I thought you might want this," said Daniel.

He put the tray down beside her, then closed the door behind him and put his lip fingers to his lip to say, 'Shush'. Although Great Aunt Mimi liked to live on simple but nutritious fayre, no expense was spared when guests came.

"I feel like a queen," said Amelia, picking up a water biscuit stacked with a big block of cheddar. Pushing her little finger out, she felt like she was one of the posh ladies she'd seen in the tea shops in Oxford.

Daniel saw a glimmer of the old Amelia return, and it gave him hope he could free her from the awful household she found herself in. He felt partly responsible for her fate since he had helped Thomas acquire her.

"The food tastes exquisite, and the company is exquisite," she confessed, blushing wildly. "Thank you."

The kindness played with her emotions. Her belly had not been full for many months, now it was fit to burst. She couldn't help but let the tears of desperation that were building up in her stinging eyes fall down her cheeks. Knowing this joyous moment would be temporary and that she would soon return to her harsh life with a bump was hard to bear.

Daniel looked at the poor little thing before him, grinning bravely between the chews and the tears.

> "I bet you must wonder if you'd have been better off if you'd stayed in the orphanage?"

> "I don't know. It's hard to say. Thomas used to say you drive yourself mad wondering about what might have been in life. Sister Nancy would probably have tried to put me in a convent or something by now, anything to calm me down," she explained with a fractured, emotional voice.

She brightened, adding:

> "I don't think I'm cut out for life as a nun, Daniel."

> "No, I don't suppose you are," he said, placing his hand on hers. "I promise I will help you, now I know how beastly it is for you to live here. You're growing up to be a fine young woman. Things will turn out alright, you'll see."

The conversation swiftly ended. Amelia's bedroom door swung open, and a thunderous Mrs Harper filled the frame, standing like Henry VIII with her hands on her hips, looking for some heads to roll.

"We will have no impropriety in this house, Mr Astley!"

"I beg your pardon, I am checking on the girl's welfare. Can't you see she's underfed? Uncared for?"

"She bides fine. Miss Beadle has given her employment and a roof over her head. If anything, she's lucky. Especially considering she came from the slums of Whitechapel. We all know how the homeless girls there make their money."

"Do you have to be that spiteful?"

"Yes, especially to a man who thinks it is acceptable to stay in this young girl's room in the evening after you've been drinking with the lady of the house. People will talk."

"Who's going to know Mrs Harper?" said Daniel. "No one unless you go blabbing with that cruel tongue of yours."

The argument made Amelia even more distraught. She collapsed into Daniel's neck and tried to hide from the world. Mrs Harper was about to explode.

"What's all this noise?" demanded Arthur Harper, huffing and puffing as he scanned the scene in Amelia's room. "Do you think it's acceptable to be in the room with Miss Sinden at this late hour? No wonder my poor wife is reprimanding you."

"He was mauling her, trying it on like some sort of hapless Casanova. Heaven knows what would have happened if I hadn't turned up!" she whined.

" I bet this little strumpet was leading him on," said Arthur.

Both Amelia and Astley were equally incensed at the suggestion.

"I was merely trying to comfort the poor girl."

"I shall have to tell Miss Beadle after breakfast," said Arthur.

"Tell her what you like. By tomorrow, I promise you, Miss Sinden will be far away from this place, and you'll never have to be disappointed in her conduct again."

"I'll be gone?" chirped Amelia with glee, sitting bolt upright after hearing the revelatory news.

"Yes," said Daniel, desperately trying to look like he had a plan but having nothing of the sort.

"I will speak to Thomas now and straighten this out."

"Will you be alright tonight, Amelia?"

Before she could answer, Mr and Mrs Harper shooed him out of the girl's quarters and locked the door.

He marched upstairs, leaving the Harpers to gossip about him in their room.

When he got upstairs, he found Thomas and Richard having a heated debate over something and nothing on the landing.

"Stop that. I have something important to discuss."

"You have?"

"Yes, let's go to the Randolph Hotel for morning coffee, I hear their biscuits and petit fours are to die for? It's been so tense tonight we've not had time to talk properly. I have an exciting proposition for you."

He walked towards his bedroom door as the other two looked on, begging for more information.

"And?" asked Richard.

"And—All good things come to those who wait, gentlemen," he said with a grin. "So, you'll be there?"

"Anything to dodge revising for my bar exams," grinned Thomas.

15

THE HORRIBLE BREAKFAST

After a horrible breakfast with Mimi snapping at them, Mr and Mrs Harper giving Daniel the evil eye, the three men were glad to be free.

"A table for three please, for morning tea," said Daniel, as they approached the opulent reception area, lit by an exquisite chandelier.

"How's the revision going, Thomas?" teased Sir Richard as they walked to their table.

"Dreadfully. If the hall sells, I will be able to avoid becoming a barrister altogether. There's no need for a place that big with the three of us rattling round in it. A few people have expressed an interest in it. It might be sold within a month, perhaps."

"And it won't have to be a lawyer forever. You can access the rest of your trust fund soon," added Daniel.

A young man in a stunning red and gold uniform walked over.

"Ah yes, I will have three pots of your best Javanese coffee, please, for my good friends here. And the cake selection. The deluxe one."

"Right you are, sir."

"Someone's feeling flush," joked Thomas as he closed the à la carte brunch menu.

"So, this proposition, what is it, old bean?" asked Richard, his curiosity getting the better of him.

"It's Amelia. Would it be fair to say you don't want to marry her, Thomas?"

"Well, I suppose you could look at it that way. I was hoping to resume her training when she was twenty. I was sure having her lodge with Great Aunt Mimi, and the Harpers would toughen her up a bit."

"So, you're expecting her to put her life on hold for three years whilst you decide if you wish to continue with this scheme of yours?"

"Well, yes and no," replied Thomas.

"Just get to the point, Daniel," snapped Wentworth.

"Well, as you know, Thomas asked me to draw up a contract with the two girls, which explained what would happen should the experiment succeed or fail. Amelia signed that contract fair and square, and apart from 'flinching' when you shot at her, I can't see what she's done wrong. She deserves the £100 you promised and help to set up the business."

"There's no need to be hasty, Daniel. I still have time to work on her."

"But I am not sure she has time. Did you see her last night by any chance?"

"No," they replied.

"Well, she's like a bag of bones. Her eye sockets were all dark and sunken, her cheeks hollow. I am sure Mr and Mrs Harper are mistreating her, and Mimi sees her so infrequently, she's not aware of it."

"Balderdash," said Richard.

"Then why was she locked in her room when I went to see her last night after dinner if she's not mistreated? I appreciate people of Mimi's generation think servants should be seen and not heard, but holding someone captive, well, it doesn't sit well with me at all. We have to do something."

The waiter staggered over to their table, laden with coffee and cake. The tray almost filled the tabletop.

"She has done what we asked of her, Thomas, and I don't see the point of pretending this experiment will ever work. It failed with Richard's son. It failed with Lucretia, and you are still a single man."

"It's time to draw a line under this and give her the money you owe her and let her move on. After the experience with you, I doubt she wants to marry any man. You are obliged to pay her off and help her set up some sort of business suitable for a woman."

Wentworth nodded.

"No one likes a chap who goes back on his word, Thomas. You must admit my son didn't develop the traits we discussed, and you didn't even threaten him with a gun."

"Shall I remind you of the key clauses from the contract? I know them off by heart?" Daniel warned.

"Alright, alright. I give in. We'll take her out of Great Aunt Mimi's employ. Then what?"

"Well, she's too young to be able to be a director of her own business, so I suggest we send her to boarding school until she is eighteen."

"She did show academic promise on occasions. What school are you thinking?"

"I am glad you agree she has potential. I suggest Roseden," said Daniel, matter-of-factly.

"But that will cost a fortune!" complained Thomas.

"A couple of years will cost a lot less than the £100 you were supposed to pay Lucretia, should she have made it to adulthood. You've got off lightly. It's the least you can do for driving a wrecking ball through Amelia's life. You have a moral duty to support that girl."

"I agree," said Sir Richard, "she deserves a proper education, Thomas, not that strange system you foisted upon her."

Begrudgingly, Thomas agreed.

"I'll send a telegram to the school and get her enrolled, then I will get Victor to collect her."

"Excellent. I'll have a chat with your Great Aunt Mimi before I return to Lincoln's Inn," said Daniel, as he passed around a plate of pink cakes. "Now, who wants one of these delightful French fancies?"

Thomas grabbed at one, and stuffed it whole in his mouth, just in case he felt the need to complain.

16

THE UNEXPECTED GUEST

"Who can that be?" complained Arthur, putting his fresh cup of tea back on its porcelain saucer. "We're not expecting any callers this morning, are we, Edith? Why people don't follow the rules and drop a calling card off in the afternoon, I'll never know. And if it's one of those blasted door-to-door salesmen, I'll wring his neck."

Arthur trekked upstairs, grizzling more with each step.

"Ah, Mr Harper. Is Miss Beadle available?"

"I shall see if she's accepting visitors this early," he drawled, making a point of staring at his pocket watch, then slowly glided towards the sitting room.

The door closed, and Daniel listened to the muffled voices with his fingers crossed. *'I'll come back after lunch if they're that hung up on protocol.'*

"Miss Beadle will see you now, Mr Astley. Follow me."

*

Back at the hotel, Richard quizzed Thomas on why his experiments kept failing.

"I have to ask, is it you or the system? Those are the two common factors," he teased.

Thomas was having none of it.

"I could get her to learn parrot fashion, of course, but I couldn't put fire in her belly. She learned all the bard's sonnets off by heart. She made a wooden rowing boat, although, thinking back, it sank when she tried to retrieve a lost oar. I suppose it's the same as saying, 'you can lead a horse to water, but you can't make it drink.' She would accept any challenge I put in front of her. But she would never challenge herself. She saw no value in stretching herself. The only thing in our favour was her desire to meet my expectations."

"And given you were quite menacing towards the end, that loyalty might be an illusion, created by fear rather than duty. That's no basis for a marriage."

Richard reached for the final cake on the fine porcelain serving tray.

"Perhaps young Victor caught her eye? Didn't you say Sarah thought he was interested in her?"

"Will you marry again, Richard?"

"Oh, I doubt it. I've had my heart broken too many times when the Lord chose to take them from me early," said the thrice widowed man. "Besides, I'm nearly seventy. The ladies want young bucks like you."

"Thank goodness you didn't propose to Amelia," said Wentworth. "It would have been a disaster. There is a girl for you out there, who will love you for who you are, warts and all."

*

Daniel paid for Amelia to stay at a simple coaching inn in Woodstock for a few days until her room at Rosedon School for Girls was ready.

Victor barely recognised her when he collected her. She was so thin. He felt immense pity for the girl and regretted not doing more to get Thomas to rein in his behaviour in those last few days in Wales. He was tormented about Lucretia. *'How might she have fared if I had spoken up for her?'* A vision of the bloodied pocket watch filled his mind's eye. Thomas had the gift's broken glass repaired, but every time Victor looked at it, he could still see the stain of death on it.

"Rosedon then, Miss Sinden?" he said politely as he helped her into the hired coach.

"Yes!" she trilled as he struggled to get her heavy wooden trunk onto the roof. "It's only for a few terms, but it will be the making of me. I just know it."

"Just remember me as you take over the world," he replied, testing the waters of her emotions.

She held his gaze with a true intensity.

"How could I forget you, Victor?"

Each time he replayed those precious words in his mind, he smiled to himself on the long five days it took to get Amelia safely to Rosedon School, nestled on the south coast. Each day, Amelia became more beautiful the more time he spent with her. As he trundled along, alone on the driver's bench, he daydreamed of them getting a job at a small country house, the two of them working together in some rural idyll for an appreciative master and mistress. At every stop, Victor had to hold his tongue and not get down on one knee. *'To hell with asking Thomas's permission first. This is what I want.'*

*

Things moved on quickly for Amelia once she entered the prestigious boarding school and for the better. Each term, it seemed life changed dramatically, not only for her but also for Thomas.

Young Miss Sinden swept into Roseden like a princess, relishing the prospect of educating herself in botany, chemistry, history, English and maths. She wrote her first letter to Thomas a few weeks after arriving.

Dear Thomas,

I am settling into Rosedon. It feels like a second home already. My education is coming on in leaps and bounds, and my teachers are astounded at how quickly I am flourishing. I am sure that is down to you nurturing my inquisitive mind. I often wonder what you would think if you could see me now, doing wonderful experiments of my own with bunsen burners in the laboratory.

I know it sounds unbelievable, but it appears I am the only former orphan from Whitechapel at this respected seat of learning!

Ah! Please forgive my momentary light-heartedness. I am so grateful that you have honoured your contract with me. It will be the making of me, I can tell already.

As a thank you, I enclose a selection of small watercolour paintings of the tropical plants I studied at Kew Gardens. They were identified by Mr Darwin on his last visit to the Galapagos Islands. I hope you like them,

Fondly,

Amelia.

Thomas broke the habit of a lifetime and wrote back.

Dearest Amelia,

Thank you for your last letter. It seems Lady Luck has smiled on me, and I can report some good fortune of my own. The old family hall in Abingdon has been sold for an excellent price. I am free of the millstone that reminded me that I, too, am an orphan now. Losing my childhood home was painful and yet freeing.

As a short-term measure, I have taken up residence in a small townhouse in Oxford, shared with some other thinkers from the Art and Science Society. I suppose I don't need to tell you I spend a lot of time there debating ideas.

I am still holding off from doing my law exams for the bar, despite Daniel insisting it will be 'good for me.' He says I am 'drifting' and 'need focus'. He's entitled to his opinion, I suppose. I can't help but feel my mental talents are best used elsewhere, but, as always, I know not where that might be.

I am delighted to hear your studies are going well and look forward to you visiting at Christmas time.

Yours,

Thomas.

Thomas had neglected to mention in his note that an older woman, a middle-aged poet called Anna, had caught his eye at the Art and Science Society. Even Daniel had noticed he was besotted with her. Secretly, Thomas considered her 'his muse', sighing as he dreamed of her when he mooched around his flat, all alone.

Anna was a very rare creature, a woman of independent means. Thomas followed her around at the cheese and wine parties. After the talks, she did like a little chihuahua, but she barely noticed he existed.

She learned of Thomas's unrequited love through one of Daniel's letters.

> *'I think Thomas has bet his shirt on the wrong horse. Anna is not interested in him at all. I don't want to gossip, but, reading between the lines, people say she has never had a romantic interest in men. I have told him as much and that he needs to move on, but you know how stubborn he can be—'*

Amelia chuckled at the image.

'Anna shares the same cold, clinical outlook on life, where everything is practical, and nothing is pleasurable. It's all quite amusing seeing the two curmudgeons putting the world to rights.'

Despite there being no romantic spark, intellectually, they were soul mates. Anna and Thomas spent a lot of time talking together about the nature of society, the role of government, free will and determinism, each giving as much as they got in the debating arena. It was through these many debates that Anna was introduced to Sir Richard when he visited Oxford.

Daniel's next note mentioned a swift change in events.

> *'It seems Richard Wentworth, recently widowed for the third time, poor chap, has proposed to Anna, and she has agreed. Thomas is furious, of course. It's put his nose out of joint. Richard says they are both looking for companionship in later life and see nothing wrong with it, but you know how stubborn Thomas can be. To atone, Anna has offered to introduce Thomas to her younger sister, Elizabeth, but he is still fuming.'*

At the Christmas holidays, Amelia visited Thomas at his new townhouse, just a few doors down from his odious Great Aunt Mimi. Everyone prayed they wouldn't bump into her in the street, especially Amelia. No one knew exactly how much Mimi was aware of Amelia's cruel treatment, locked in the basement for the best part of a year, but everyone suspected she must have known something.

Throughout the festive season, Thomas's house was filled with joy as the old friends gathered together. As they saw in the New Year, Thomas, Daniel, Sarah, and Victor all raised a toast to Amelia and wished her well in her studies.

On her Easter visit, Amelia discovered Thomas was quite smitten with Elizabeth. Like Anna, she was another feisty, independent woman. Sir Richard had arranged for Elizabeth to start an administrative post at the university, processing undergraduate applications and paperwork. It seemed Richard had bought her a new gizmo, 'a type-writer'. Mastering the device was a wonderful route into well-paid office work for a young woman, and it offered a high degree of independence as a career.

Elizabeth's well-educated and free-spirited mind was drawn to Thomas and his robust rejection of what polite society expected a person to do. From a distance, she had delighted in his curious lifestyle, strange opinions, and bookish nature. Unlike Thomas, Elizabeth was also blessed with a sense of fun. One evening, after a society lecture, after a little too much wine, she hinted at an attraction to Thomas. He nearly fell out of his favourite armchair at the news.

> "You're always so academic, Thomas. Have you ever thought of going to Paris to take up painting? Those impressionists bucking the trend of what's expected in the art world seem like your sort of chaps? Or learning to play tennis? Or dancing the waltz?"

> "No, I most certainly have not, Miss #Surname. Those pursuits are hideous. Far too effeminate."

He gave up protesting when he saw that Elizabeth wasn't going to take no for an answer, and he had to admit, the more time he spent debating with her, the more he was drawn to her.

On his return from a month in Paris, he explained his reasoning for the trip in a drunken conversation with Richard.

"Firstly, it delays having to study for those wretched law exams, and secondly, I hope that once I can parry with a sabre or serenade her below her window, I'll have a fighting chance of her getting her to marry me."

Richard was tickled pink that Thomas couldn't see the irony that his beloved was moulding him to be the husband she wanted, rather than him shaping her. He couldn't have been more out of control of his quest for a bride if he'd tried. *'How times have changed since you left the mission with two orphans and Giseau's textbook!'*

Daniel loved to tease him about being hen-pecked too.

"I finally found a woman who is my equal, Daniel, and all you can do is ridicule me for it."

"Does she make you happy, Thomas?"

"Wonderfully so," he sighed wistfully.

"Well, isn't that all that matters really?"

Thomas gave an out of character wry smile as he had no option but to agree.

The following Christmas, when she returned home, Amelia was filled in on all the latest developments over lunch with Thomas, Daniel, Sarah, and Victor.

"Last week, at the theatre, Elizabeth secretly proposed to Thomas when she tired of waiting for him to pop the question. It was most amusing," said Sarah.

Putting down his knife and fork, Daniel gave a hearty laugh and spluttered:

"Well, he did say he wanted a strong woman. It certainly looks like he's got one!"

"Victor asked Thomas if 'he liked being hen-pecked yesterday. You should have heard the language!" added Sarah. "'He's even off to a pantomime at the Theatre Royal with his lady friend next week."

Daniel pretended to be so shocked he needed to steady himself on a table. Thomas kicked Victor in the shins.

"Ow, that hurt," he complained.

"It was supposed to!"

"That's enough about me. What's happening with your love life, then Daniel? Is there anyone special?" asked Thomas.

"I'm far too busy with my work, for all that," he said coyly.

After the meal, the others left the table, leaving Thomas and Daniel to chat alone.

"I think Victor has a soft spot for young Amelia," said Thomas. "She has blossomed into a lovely young woman," added Daniel.

"He talks of nothing else when she is due to visit. That and the time they built a shelter for Spike in

Wales. If I mention her name, his cheeks go redder than a Mr Punch puppet on Blackpool Beach."

"You shouldn't tease him, Thomas. It's most unbecoming. Changing the subject, does Amelia know what she wants to do when she leaves Rosedon? Has she said anything?"

"Not a dickie bird. Perhaps she will be suited to university? Royal Holloway might be just the ticket. What do you think?"

Daniel gave a non-committal smile. If he could wave a magic wand, he wanted Amelia to join his practice at Lincoln's Inn Fields, to run the back office and the typing pool. There were more plans, but he had to get her to agree to that first.

*

The next time they would all meet up would be Thomas and Elizabeth's wedding day. Amelia travelled up from boarding school to be their bridesmaid. Daniel was the best man and Victor chief usher. Thomas had wanted something quiet and understated, but his bride-to-be wanted something more lavish. They had compromised with a quiet mid-afternoon service for close friends and family at St Barnabas' Church and a raucous reception with a hundred guests in the evening at the Randolph.

Amelia almost upstaged the bride in her gorgeous pastel blue dress. The epitome of understated elegance, her hair was pinned up neatly, showing her slender neck, with a few tendrils of curls draped down to soften the look. Victor was supposed to be helping the late-running guests to their church seats, but when she arrived with Elizabeth, he struggled to take his eyes off her. Sarah watched her young nephew like a hawk, wondering if today might be the day he made his move. He wouldn't be the first young man to propose to his beloved at a friend's wedding.

Daniel and Thomas stood before the altar, nervously awaiting Elizabeth, now over five minutes late. Thomas was soon put out of his misery as the organist played the first stuttering octet of notes that began Mendelsohn's Wedding March, signalling her arrival. They turned to look at the young woman, given away by Sir Richard and assisted by the lovely Amelia.

"She looks stunning," said Daniel breathlessly.

"That's my future wife you're fawning over," said Thomas giving his friend a cheeky sideways glance.

*

The lunch was the usual mix of speeches, formal toasts, and traditions. Everyone agreed the wedding cake was delicious, but it would be at the evening festivities when people let their hair down. Thomas had regretted offering to foot the drinks bill as he got a tap on the shoulder from the Maître d' saying was it alright if they put on another barrel of ale and five more cases of wine.

"I shall be mortgaging my house again at this rate, Daniel. These hotel prices here are astronomical!" complained Thomas.

"Stop being so miserly. If you can't celebrate today, when can you celebrate? Live a little. I intend to!"

The ballroom was flooded by the sound of the chamber orchestra, playing a lively selection of polkas and barn dance music.

"Do you mind if I reclaim my husband," asked Elizabeth, grabbing Thomas by the hand.

The bride and groom took the first dance, moving in perfect time to the melody. Thomas's friends looked on agog, clapping along to the rhythm.

"Has he been possessed by the devil, Amelia? Made some sort of Faustian pact?" whispered Daniel, with a grin.

To the other side of her, feeling left out, Victor vied for her attention.

"Don't they make a lovely couple? I am glad Thomas has found his soulmate after all."

Later as everyone danced, Daniel managed to partner himself up with Amelia for a lively waltz. They floated and spun around the sprung wooden floor like a pair of professionals. Daniel was surprised he could keep in time. His mind was so distracted thinking, *'just ask her!'*

The music stopped, and Daniel took a moment to get his breath. Amelia felt a hand tenderly squeeze her shoulder.

"Will you come and help Elizabeth out of her wedding dress?" asked Sarah. "They are leaving on their honeymoon soon."

"Of course, excuse me, Daniel."

He gave her a nod as the courage he had carefully plucked up to propose melted away.

Anna, Sarah, and Amelia helped the beautiful bride change into her going-away outfit. A royal blue dress and shawl with black beaded lace trimming.

"There must be a hundred buttons on the back of this thing!" grizzled Sarah as their aching fingers all fought to do them up.

"A toast! To my beautiful sister," said Anna, raising a champagne flute in the air as the others gently clinked their flutes alongside.

There was a knock at the door, and a man's voice asked:

"Are you decent, Mrs Beadle?"

"Yes, come in, Victor," said Sarah with a laugh.

"Can I collect your luggage, please, Elizabeth. Master Thomas is out already waiting at the front for you. I think he's had enough socialising for one day. He's not really cut out for it. He was muttering about wanting to be rid of everyone."

"Is he pacing, Victor? He always paces when he is about to snap," quizzed Elizabeth.

"No, he's not pacing. He's talking to Daniel. Well, Daniel's talking at Thomas, who is just standing there with his hands in his pockets, nodding occasionally. I doubt he's listening to a word."

"Right then. This is it. My first night of married life. I'm ready."

She swept out of the room looking magical, with Anna and Sarah following behind.

"Shall I get a bell boy to help you with that case, Victor? It looks like it weighs a ton."

"Oh, that's fine. I'll sort it."

"Alright, but let me get you a nightcap at the end of the evening at least? You've been run ragged today. You've earned it. Thomas will be paying, so why not have a nice Armagnac," Amelia chuckled.

"You're on. Thank you. You will come and see me, won't you?"

"I promise."

When Amelia finally made it back to the party, Daniel was looking for her.

"There you are! Have you got a moment?"

She nodded as he escorted her by the arm gently towards a private little space, amongst the throng, an offset bay window lined with plush red velvet curtains. As she turned round to face him, he reached into his suit pocket. Her gaze was drawn to a scarlet velvet box, complete with a sparkling engagement ring.

"So, will you marry me, Amelia Sinden?" Daniel pleaded with his most charming of smiles.

"Yes! Yes!" said Amelia, jumping up and down on her tiptoes, clapping her dainty hands. "Of course, I will."

The couple had grins so broad they would struggle to get out of the hotel's grand doors.

"Oh, but what about Thomas? Does he mind? He's like my step-father."

"I spoke to him before he left. He's delighted," Daniel reassured as he slid the ring onto her ring finger. "A perfect fit, wouldn't you say?"

She stood on her tiptoes again and gave him the faintest of kisses on the cheek, then looked straight into his dark eyes.

"Perfect," she murmured as she craned towards him.

As her gaze fell from his face, it focused on the carriage clock.

"Gosh, is that the time? Ten to twelve! The midnight hour is almost upon us!" she said, fidgeting. "Do you mind if I say goodnight to Victor? I promised I would."

"If there's one thing Thomas drummed into you over the years, it's the importance of keeping your word. Go on, run along now. I can manage a few minutes without you. We have the rest of our lives together!" he said with a wink.

"I hope you won't always be that corny!" Amelia teased as her eyes hunted the room for Victor.

"You look exhausted, young man."

"Thank you for coming over."

Victor gave a young waiter a nod, and he glided over, bringing a small drinks tray with a sherry for Amelia and a brandy for him.

As she reached for the glass, Victor noticed the sparkling new engagement ring. It was like the hardest punch to the gut he had ever had, yet no one had laid a finger on him. He decided not to ask about who the lucky man was. It would hurt too much.

2040 - 8502

17

ROSEDEN

Towards the end of Amelia's final term at Rosedon, the hall master paid a visit to her room. On opening the door, he greeted her cheerfully, peering above a large parcel.

"A present for you, I believe, Miss Sinden."

"That's odd. I am not expecting anything. What can it be?" she said gleefully, running her hands over the expanse of smooth brown paper.

She gave it a sniff and a gentle shake, but no more information was forthcoming.

"Not a clue. Thank you, Mr Hargreaves. I shall let you know what it is."

Putting the package on her desk, she carefully teased open the wrapping. Inside was another cardboard box, with some bold lettering printed on it.

Miles M. Bartholomew's Patented Stenograph. Illinois USA

'A steno- what?'

On the reverse side, it said:

A machine for writing shorthand

Amelia had no idea what a stenograph might be, or short-hand for that matter, and had to open the box to find out more. Inside was a perfectly smooth wooden case. Resting on that was a handwritten note from Daniel. Sliding it out of the envelope, it read:

> *"I hope you like this. If you can get the hang of it,*
> *there's an office job for you at my legal practice*
> *taking notes as I interview clients.'*

Lifting the lid, she looked at the funny little machine with its ten fanned-out keys and pressed a few. Nonplussed, she dismissed it as some sort of cut-price typewriter. Looking for an instruction manual, she spotted a roll of paper.

She fed it through the mechanism and jabbed at a few keys. Little black marks appeared on the paper. None of them was legible. It was as if it was a secret code.

'Has Daniel started representing the Masons?' she pondered with a grin.

Underneath the hardwood footplate of the little mechanical keyboard was a concise single-page instruction manual. She lay back on her bed and began to read. Daniel was a clever man who always had her best interests at heart, so she owed it to him to not be so dismissive of what the thing might be capable of.

> *From the Desk of Miles Bartholomew, Court Re-*
> *porter,*

Congratulations on purchasing this high-quality shorthand machine. It revolutionises human typing speed from 120 words per minute with a traditional keyboard to 350 words per minute when used by a trained operator.

The manual went on to point out several key features.

'Well, I never! This is perfect for the job. I just hope I measure up.'

Looking at the picture on the box, Amelia began to assemble the little tool. First, she lifted a thin metal strut at the back of the unit and put a narrow reel of paper tape onto its spool. She rotated it with her finger to check it spun freely and wouldn't misfeed. *'Good. What's next?'* Then she took the end of the paper and fed it through a metal guide rail at the centre. It slid through the mechanism as smoothly as a hot knife through butter. She fed the end into another reel that looked like it would gather up the tape as it was completed.

She peered over the round keys. They were laid out like Elizabeth's typewriter, with the finger pads at the front and some converging metal levers at the back, but, curiously, none of the keys had anything written on them. She pressed one. A little black line, like a hyphen, appeared on the paper. She pressed another key. It left a line behind too. It was more like morse code than printed letters a typewriter would produce.

'Hmm'

Flipping over the instruction card, it all became clear. A simple list of five-character codes, made up of gaps or marks, was a short code for the letters of the alphabet, a few common syllables like **qu,ch,sh,th** and the numbers **0** to **9**. She pressed two keys together. Instead of the metal strikers colliding and getting stuck like a traditional typewriter, two marks were made. *'How clever. So much more efficient than hunting for a key and pecking at it like a chicken with one finger or teasing the letters apart. Touché, Mr Bartholomew.'*

She put her hands above the keyboard and drummed her fingers in the air to loosen them up. Then after skimming her eye down the column for the letter she needed, she typed in the code. It was slow going to begin with, but as she learned the cypher, her speed improved.

Worried she was running low on paper tape, she wrote a stenograph message and posted it to Daniel the next day.

'Thank you for your kind job offer. I accept.'

Three months later, Amelia found herself with a small flat in London and a well-paid job as a stenographer.

Not everyone in the practice was delighted to see that Daniel Astley had installed his fiancée as a clerk, but they couldn't deny that her fingers were nimble and her transcriptions accurate and that it saved them a lot of time taking notes longhand when they were dealing with their casework. But that didn't stop the naysayers actively trying to undermine her.

Some of Daniel's more traditional colleagues thought a woman's place was in the home, for all jobs except, at a push, being a telephone exchange operator, and their small chambers didn't need one of those. But Daniel, a forward thinking-man, strongly disagreed and felt stenography would be a blessing for them.

At the end of a trying week, when Daniel felt he could have herded cats more successfully than manage their gloomy opinions, things came to a head.

"What about client confidentiality, Daniel? Can she be trusted not to blab?"

"I beg your pardon?"

"Well, she'll listen to a lot of commercial and personal details. We don't want anything leaked. It would kill our credibility. How do we know she's not been planted here by a rival firm?"

"The thing is, Gerald, this is my practice, and I have the final say. And as for loyalty, agreeing to be my wife is about the biggest gesture of loyalty Miss Sinden could make to me. I have no fears about that. We are going to adopt this new technology, and you are going to like it. Is that understood?"

Gerald nodded his head but decided, like many a trade union leader, that work-to-rule was the only way to get his dissenting voice heard. Always in demand, Astley looked at his watch, sighed and headed off to another important meeting, leaving Gerald to poison the minds of his colleagues.

> "Here's how we shall handle this," he said, closing the door as he briefed his devious little cabal. "I think Daniel needs to remember we are partners here too."

Amelia couldn't understand why, even with practice, recording the client conversations was getting trickier. Sadly, in her eagerness to impress, she hadn't picked up on the subtle changes in their behaviour. They would deliberately mumble, pepper concepts liberally with Latin or add in other unfamiliar legal jargon when speaking, then say she had made transcription errors. When she attended client meetings, they did their best to speak faster than she could key in the words. Sometimes, they would say her services weren't needed, and they would make their own (more accurate) notes, but would she mind fetching some teas or coffees for their clients. The days were becoming long, frustrating, and mentally draining for the poor girl as she continued to feel outnumbered and undermined by their nastiness.

The lowest point had been when she had tripped, bringing in a tray of drinks, spilling the coffee on some important paperwork, and of course, it had to be Gerald's. Like a big fat angry walrus, he stormed off to Daniel's office with the ruined records, slamming the door behind him for extra dramatic effect. He made sure he yelled loudly so that everyone in the building could hear him slating Amelia for her 'lack of professionalism' and the 'irreparable damage' she had caused to his case.

"That's enough. I'll deal with it, Gerald," bellowed Daniel.

A bereft Amelia watched Daniel, blinkered by fury, march straight past her without a word. He strode over to Essex Street and The Little Cheshire Cheese pub, where he stayed for two hours.

"You might as well go home, Miss Sinden. He's going to sack you, fiancée or not." hissed Gerald with pride.

In tears, Amelia grabbed her hat and coat from the stand and made her way back to her little Hampstead bolt hole, where she slammed the door on the world, then felt her body slide down its glossy paintwork as she fell in a sobbing heap on the floor. Daniel arrived later that afternoon smelling of drink. Amelia was hysterical as he forced his way in. It took a lot of persuasion to calm her down.

"Listen to me," he said, shaking her by the shoulders. "Listen, damn you."

"Please don't hurt me!" she protested.

"Hurt you? Why on earth would I do that? Sit down and just listen!"

"You've been in the pub all afternoon. I've let you down."

"If you will let me finish," he said, giving her the evil eye, "yes, I was in the pub, but I was with the High Court usher."

She looked bemused.

"And he's agreed to take you on as a stenographer. With 320 words a minute, you will be their most skilled operator."

"So, no more Gerald?"

"No more Gerald. I promise. And you'll get a pay rise too, as it's a more high-profile position."

A week later, Amelia found herself walking into the high court with her head held high. A few days later, when Gerald came to defend his case in Count Number One, she gave him her best 'Yes, it's me' glare.

Finally, things were going well for Amelia after a bumpy transition from Rosedon into adult life. Thanks to her strict upbringing at the mission and with Thomas, she was used to living on next to nothing, so her white-collar salary stretched a long way, so much so, she was able to save a lot of it. Better still, she didn't need to touch the final payment that Thomas gave her as part of their contract coming to an end. With savings in the bank and her forthcoming wedding to Daniel, life couldn't get any better.

They were married a year to the day after Daniel proposed. This time the roles would be reversed, Thomas the best man, and Elizabeth the bridesmaid. The venue was

Temple Church, a venue so prestigious the vicar needed a special dispensation from the Archbishop of Canterbury to hold the service. Amelia wondered what Sister Nancy would make of that when she read the announcement in the newspaper.

Amelia gave up her little flat, and they moved into a new home, still in leafy Hampstead. It was quite small, only big enough for the two of them, but it was a happy little home. That was until a delighted Amelia revealed to Daniel she was expecting their first child.

> "I can't believe how much my life has turned around," Amelia confessed to Sarah when she visited. "Here I am, a wife and soon to be a mother. Daniel says I need to give up work soon and rest, but I quite like being busy, else I start dreading what the birth will be like if I rattle around here on my own."
>
> "But you're not on your own. You have Daniel?"
>
> "Yes, but he's working terribly long hours at the moment. He leaves well before seven in the morning and returns at gone nine most nights. I worry about him taking on too much trying to grow the practice."
>
> "I can't believe you're having a bairn. You're not much past a bairn yourself," said Sarah.

Amelia stroked her belly gently, bursting with maternal pride.

"If it's a boy, we're going to call it Thomas," she said. "And if it's a girl, we will call it Sarah after you."

"Who wants a tea," asked Victor, who still couldn't quite bring himself to think of Amelia with another man.

*

By their second anniversary, Daniel was still working long hours, taking on more high-profile commercial cases. The details in the contracts were complicated, and putting the case together was becoming more draining. He couldn't relax. One silly mistake could undo all the hard work the practice had done to build a solid reputation. One night when their son was bawling his heart out, Amelia came down to the study and found Daniel was still working.

"Looks like all three of us will get no sleep."

Daniel was at his wit's end, running his fingers through his hair, his brow feverish, his mind scatty. He knew he needed to focus, but he was too exhausted to do so. Amelia bounced young Thomas on her hip, trying to comfort the child just as much as her husband. The lad began to tire and snuggled his face into the curve of her neck and shoulder.

"These endless late nights, Daniel. They're no good for you. You need rest. You've not taken a holiday in nearly two years. You need a break. You're a man, not a machine. There comes a point where you ask, is this worth it? We have enough to get by on, don't we?"

"Perhaps," he said, scanning the papers, not really listening.

She laid little Thomas in a Moses basket, then sat on his desk and lifted his hands from the papers, then asked:

"What would you really like to do?"

"I have no idea. Not this," he said. "That's all I do know."

"How about we move out to the country? Live a quiet life? Perhaps not as frugal as Thomas in Abingdon, but not with all the trappings and noise of London. "I would love the freedom of the rolling hills and for us to spend time together as a family. You don't have to do your legal work in Temple? I mean, there are other options?"

"I could do something nice and easy like property conveyancing or wills. I can't remember the last time I saw a pile of contract paperwork less than three inches thick," he groaned.

"A will is a few sheets of foolscap, even for the most affluent people, isn't it? Would you get much for selling your share in the business?"

"Thank you, my love," he said, squeezing her hand. "I can be so blind at times. Some money will be due, but as to how much, I don't know. The others in chambers don't work anywhere near as many hours as me. It's all boozy lunches and long meetings out of the office. Unless they are actually in court, I honestly don't know what half of them do."

"So, that's decided then? You stop being a high-flying City of London lawyer, and you'll help sort out country bumpkins arguing about who owns a fence?"

"If it makes you happy, my dear, then yes, why not."

"Are you coming up to bed? It's nearly three in the morning."

"Soon, once this is all straight," he apologised, rubbing his aching head.

18

AMELIA'S PROJECT

As Daniel tied up the loose ends with his business, Amelia was busy with a project of her own. Her push to relocate to the country had a second thread, a project close to her own heart.

Last month at court, she had been covering a case that referenced Dr Barnardo. He was in hot water for sending children for a fresh start in Canada, with some parents complaining it had been against their will, angry that they had subsequently lost contact with their children. The case had given her a grounding in setting up an orphanage, the perfect business for a rural area, and she was sure her establishment would help the children thrive.

One day, the judge had adjourned the court unexpectedly. Taking advantage of the unexpected leisure time, Amelia had gone to see Reverend Bennett and asked for his advice on setting up an orphanage. Thomas Beadle's strange idea of imparting missing knowledge into thirsty minds piqued her interest, and she was sure she could help underprivileged city children get off to a good start in the country. Simeon had been instrumental in arranging the facilities and staff at the Deserving Women's Christian Mission, and he sat on many philanthropic committees that had set up others too.

"Well, I must say, you have progressed a lot since you left here, Amelia. I remember you being a little tearaway, always arguing with that other girl, what was her name—"

"Lucretia—?"

"Yes, Lucretia. Terrible business what happened to her, running away from Sir Wentworth like that. Still, it worked out better for you, didn't it, now the wife of a lawyer who works in Temple."

"Yes, we met at the Art and Science Society when I accompanied Sir Richard to a lecture one night, and the rest is history, I suppose? We grew to love each other over the years. We have a son, Thomas Richard."

Amelia hoped the little white lie would slip into Simeon's mind undetected.

"I always said the Lord works in mysterious ways, and your story is a case in point, Mrs Astley," he said with a smile. "If anyone can help orphans rise up in life, I know you can. I suggest you find a suitable property then let me know. This report will help."

He fished around in a tall set of office drawers and pulled out an envelope with everything she would need to know.

"Here," he said, handing the report to her. "Oh, and Mrs Astley?"

"Yes—" she replied with a concerned look.

"I wish you the best of luck with your project."

Amelia devoured every word on the way home on the Finchley omnibus and couldn't wait to discuss it with Daniel. *'He's a remarkable father, and he'll be a wonderful surrogate father too.'*

After a long stroll around the Heath, reading the report and chewing the fat of their future arrangements, the couple agreed. They would flee to a far-flung corner of England's green and pleasant land. Daniel would do low-key bread-and-butter legal work, and she would set up and run the orphanage.

At the next team meeting at chambers, Daniel announced his departure.

"Item number one on the agenda is who would like my shares?"

Gerald snapped them up, paying slightly over the odds just so he was guaranteed to be free of Astley for good. Before the ink had barely dried on the deal, the irascible old walrus had waddled into Daniel's office and swapped the nameplates for the senior partner to his own without discussing it with the other men left behind. As the heavy oak doors swung behind him, Daniel was glad to be free of the place. With the money he'd just received from Gerald, plus Amelia's savings, plus the final payoff from Thomas, they were very much set for life.

The news they were financially secure couldn't have come at a better time. Amelia discovered later that day that she was pregnant again, this time with twins.

When Daniel got home, Amelia laid out some details of properties in Cambridgeshire which looked suitable.

> "This one looks a little big for our needs, my love. Five bedrooms? We don't have guests often?"

They are not for guests, she said, stroking her belly. Daniel's eyebrows rose as the penny dropped.

> "They think it's twins. So, five rooms will be ideal."

Daniel mopped his brow at the thought of more sleepless nights. *'Even with a nursemaid or nanny, three children under the age of five will be character building".*

> "I thought we were moving to the country to enjoy a slower pace of life?" he said, staring into space imagining a sea of screaming faces and steaming pans filled with soiled nappies.

> "We are. It will be perfect. You're perfect."

She kissed him on the nose and went to make some tea. Daniel rubbed his head again, wondering what she would do next to perplex him. She returned with a glorious tray of refreshments.

> "Why Cambridge, Amelia? Why not anywhere?"

"Oh, Tynedale Hall, the place Reverend Bennett set up in Whitechapel. It's run in partnership with Cambridge University, so they have links there. The dons come to get a taste of real life. Simeon always jokes they learn a lot more in a week at the sharp end with the working classes than they do in three years with the gentrified."

Daniel grinned. He, too, had learned a lot from Amelia about how the other half live.

"Simeon says he will help me set up the property. But it's up to me to organise the teaching and the accommodation for the orphans. I would love to give more girls like me the opportunity to escape the East End with its drink and dead-end factory work. Does that sound mad, Daniel?"

"It sounds honourable and wanting to lift those girls up and give them a chance, to make them as strong and as powerful as they can be. I am sure Thomas will be delighted when he knows of your plans. We must invite him over as soon as we're settled. Who knows, I might even give up practising law. I don't think reading, 'riting and 'rithmetic will pose too much of a problem to an Oxford graduate like me."

The arduous job of packing up their belongings began.

"It's amazing how much stuff we've accumulated in the two years we've been here," said Amelia as she watched Daniel fill up another box of books. "I wish I could help more. You look exhausted."

"You just concentrate on looking after those little ones. Never mind lugging our possessions around. The removal men will help on the day."

Their pretty new house in Grantchester, just south of Cambridge, was even more delightful than their three-storey townhouse in Hampstead.

They trundled up the lane to their new home and school-house, smiling from ear to ear. In the warm afternoon sun, the buildings looked lovely and welcoming.

One of the removal's men, Bill, hopped down from the wagon and asked what to unpack first.

"Er, that box there, the tea chest. That has the door keys in it and some of our essentials. Candles, mugs, tea and the kettle."

Fred was trying to tie up their horse to a gatepost and not paying attention.

"Fred! Fred!" yelled Bill. "I don't know, Mr Astley. He's as deaf as a post, Fred, when he wants to be."

"Here, pass the chest down. I'll get it inside for Amelia. She'll be parched after the long journey."

Bill heaved the box to the edge of the cart and lifted it over the lip. Daniel raised his hands.

"Got it?"

"Aye, you can let go now."

The weight of it took Daniel by surprise. He tensed his abdomen to protect his back and huffed and puffed as he strained to control the box. His heart thumped in his chest, and blood swooshed in his ears.

Suddenly, he had a searing pain in his head, like his brain was on fire. He lost control of his left side, and within a split second, he had collapsed.

"Daniel," screamed Amelia.

She ran to him and knelt down.

"Take little Thomas," she yelled to Bill, terrified, standing still as a statue with his mouth open. "Take the boy, now!"

Bill clutched the lad close to him and made sure the tot faced the other way. Amelia collapsed to the floor, desperate to do something with her unresponsive husband. He slapped his cheek, shook him by the shoulder, but there was nothing. His face looked odd, like it was a Madame Tussaud model that had begun to melt. It drooped, and it scared her.

"He looks like my grandad did once. Doctor said it was a stroke or summin. You'd better get help."

Bill handed the child onto Fred and took the horse into Grantchester at breakneck speed. Amelia was getting more distraught, yelling into her husband's ear.

"Stay with me, Daniel. You hear me. That was the deal. We live happily ever after, here in this house. Stay. With. Me."

His pulse was weak and erratic, his breath rasping, but Amelia clung onto that for all she was worth.

By the time the doctor arrived, it was too late. Daniel had gone to the Lord.

While Amelia waited for the undertaker to arrive, tearful, clutching onto her son, Fred and Bill trooped in and out, dropping off the couple's belongings in silence.

19

THE CRUEL FRESH START

Amelia was devastated to send a telegram to Thomas revealing that her husband and his oldest, closest friend had suddenly passed away. Their first visit to the house was supposed to be a joyous experience. Now, they were helping to arrange the funeral of a loved one, insisting that they would rally round to help.

When they arrived first thing the next morning, Amelia had not slept and looked as pale as a ghost herself.

"Oh, you poor thing, everything's still in boxes," said Sarah the minute she arrived. "Victor and I will get this all straight. You sort out the arrangements with Thomas and Elizabeth."

Amelia gave a faint smile of gratitude.

"I've got some bread and butter with me in a hamper. I don't suppose you've eaten either?"

She shook her head and bit her lip to stop more tears from falling. Nibbling at the crusts, it was slow going with no appetite.

"If you won't eat for you, then you'll have to eat for this little 'un,'" said Victor, stroking the lad's hair, choking up as the tiny little hands gripped onto him, desperate for the comfort of human touch.

Victor leaned in to whisper in the infant's tiny ear.

"I lost my dad when I was about your age. Life can be so bloomin' rotten. Really rotten. You're a bit young to be learning that, ain't ya. But it's not always horrible. Some bits of life, well, they're magical. There will be lots of days to come that will make you smile and feel like a king. And your mother, well, she's got a great big heart, and she can love you enough for two. I promise you that, little fella."

The biggest bell at St Andrew and St Mary's church rang out, with three steady, deep rings, over and over, a 'passing bell,' signalling to the villagers that a man had left this mortal coil, each of them hoping it wasn't for their father or grandfather. No curtains could be drawn, or clocks stopped. They were all in the crates in the hall.

20

THE SERVICE

The funeral was arranged for seven days hence, at the quaint parish church, not far from the River Cam. It was a lovely restful setting, and Mr Cottam promised the day would go smoothly. Amelia dreaded the thought of her beloved husband lying alone at the chapel of rest but lacked the courage to be with him. She dreaded risking remembering him with his slumped slit of a mouth and hooded, sunken eyelids, seeing the effects of the stroke that struck him down every time she closed her eyes. She wanted to recall the happy smiling face she had loved so much.

As a mark of respect, Thomas put an announcement in The Times.

To the Friends of Daniel Astley, Esq, formerly of Hampstead Heath,

The favour of your company is requested at 11am on Friday, 17th of May, to attend the funeral of the late Daniel Astley at St Michael and St Mary's Church. Mourners will assemble at the family home, Dove Cottage, Grantchester. A wake will be held at the family home afterwards. Flowers to Mr G. Cottam (undertaker) High St Grantchester, Cambs.

News spread fast, and soon a telegram had arrived from Reverend Bennett.

Such sad news. Stop. Will attend service. Stop. Let me know how I can help. Stop.

The mourners assembled at the house wearing capes and hatbands supplied by Mr Cottam. As close relatives and friends, Amelia, Thomas, Sarah, and Victor also wore matching black kid gloves. A black crepe cross hung on the bright white door of the cottage; a door Daniel never passed through alive. Thomas and Victor greeted the people as they arrived. Some knew Daniel. Others were neighbours who never got the chance. Each person was given a mourner's card, all organised by Mr Cottam, of course. In ornate copperplate writing, it read:

Daniel Astley, aged 27

Left this earth 10 May 1895

Laid to rest 17 May 1895 (Grave 15a)
St Michael and St Margaret's Church

He heals the broken-hearted and binds up their wounds.

Psalm 147:3

Mr Cottam whispered in Thomas's ear. Six pallbearers, including Victor, Thomas, and Reverend Bennett, walked solemnly into the cottage and collected the coffin, brightly polished with silver handles. They processed to the front coach in the cortege, the bystanders taking off their hats and bowing their heads, then carefully, respectfully, they moved it into position.

The close mourners took their places in the carriages, pulled by the customary black horses with black-plumed headdresses. The grim procession made its way down the gently sloped lane and then headed left to the church.

With the coffin in position, the service began, first with some choral chanting, then some passages from the bible ready by the minister.

> "I am the resurrection and the life, sayeth the Lord: he that believeth in me, though he were dead, yet shall he live: and whosoever liveth and believeth in me shall never die."

Amelia began to sob quietly from behind her veil. *'But he is dead'* Sarah grabbed her hand and squeezed it until it ached.

The minister read a lesson and the eulogy that Amelia had written, and the choir sang a chorale as the congregation processed out of the church to the graveside, where the minister made a grim address.

> "We brought nothing into this world, and it is certain we can carry nothing out. The Lord gave, and the Lord hath taken away; blessed be the name of the Lord. For as much as it hath pleased Almighty God of his great mercy to take unto himself the soul of our dear brother here

departed: we, therefore, commit his body to the ground; earth to earth, ashes to ashes, dust to dust; in sure and certain hope of the resurrection to eternal life, through our Lord, Jesus Christ."

Handfuls of earth thudded on the coffin lid. Single flowers thrown by the ladies floated down, losing leaves and petals, as they were buffeted by the drop and the clods of soil raining down.

Finally, the ceremony was over, and Amelia didn't have to be outwardly brave for much longer. The wake would soon be over, and then she could hide in a corner and sob until her tears ran dry. How would she cope living alone in the shell of a home, a goal but no business, and two little ones on the way? Under those circumstances, she felt entitled to cry.

21

THE SHOW MUST GO ON

In the morning, Amelia woke to see little Thomas in his cot, sleeping peacefully. Downstairs she greeted Sarah and Victor cleaning up the pots and pans from the wake. She thought no one had heard her weeping in the night, but she was wrong. Sarah had checked on her every hour on the hour. With an ear pressed to her door, Sarah heard her friend's despair.

"You look pale, dear. Here let me make you a strong cup of tea. Is there any bread leftover from yesterday, Victor?"

"I can't face any food."

"Don't be silly. You need to keep your strength up, for you and little Thomas."

Amelia's expression took a turn for the worse.

"Little 'uns," she said, putting a hand on her abdomen. "Twins," she added bleakly.

"Oh, my dear child. You're still a youngster yourself. Well, try not to worry. Thomas says he is named as Daniel's executor, so he'll handle the estate. And there's plenty of rooms here. We'll all stay and get you shipshape."

Amelia started to cry again.

"You pull yourself together. You're a mother now. You can't just crumple. If anyone has the strength to carry on, build the orphanage Daniel would have been proud of—that you will be proud of—it's you. You are the fiercest, toughest woman I know. And Elizabeth can have her moments."

The poor girl's tear-streaked cheeks rounded with a faint smile.

"Reverend Bennett is taking Thomas into Cambridge to make a start on sorting out the estate. You'll be needing that money for this place, and you and your lad."

"I don't deserve this kindness," she whispered.

"Nonsense. Master Thomas, Me, Victor, when we took you from the mission, we promised to look after you until you were married or independent. Well, it's not worked out as planned with marriage—may God rest Daniel's soul—but by golly, you will be cared for."

Victor slid a cup of tea in front of her and gave her hand a comforting squeeze.

"There's an extra sugar in it for you. Just the way you like it."

One sip and Amelia felt her stomach revolt and her throat lurch. The hot dribble of liquid quickly cooled in her mouth, and she swallowed it down with a hasty gulp, hoping it would stay down. She left it a while before trying again.

The first few days of widowhood passed round in a blur filled with pain and obligation. Everyone's fussing, checking, consoling, asking, cheering, feeding, taking over, and giving her space was exhausting for the young pregnant mother. She was glad when a few more glimmers of normality filled her day. The last thing she wanted to do was forget Daniel, he was her everything, but she didn't want to be on show at her first proper trip to Grantchester or, worse, Cambridge. There was little chance of her grief being undetected—the black widow's garb would see to that, that week and for the next twelve months.

Sarah had organised her the standard crepe outfit with help from Mr Cottam. It hung up on a picture rail in her bedroom, raven black and limp, like the grim reaper was stalking her, taunting her. It was so out of character with the cheerful clothing she used to wear. The first time she approached little Thomas in it, he screamed.

As always, with a death in the family, standing still is never an option. Life goes on is not an empty platitude to cheer the bereaved. Banks needed informing, lawyers needed meeting, the deceased's possessions needed sorting before the heart wrenching clear out of beloved things that will never be used again. On top of all that, Amelia had extra pressure. Her orphanage dream would not begin operation without a mountain of work laying the foundations for it. The guilt of knowing she could help other orphans but wasn't gnawed at her. She reflected on her time at the mission, with Sister Nancy's endless, mindless chores, sewing mountains of dull grey coal sacks to earn their keep, the strict Sunday School sermons to give them moral fibre, followed by learning archaic passages from the bible to recite at morning assembly.

The one thing Thomas's ludicrous experiment had taught her was that young people are capable of far more than they, and others, give them credit for. Even if her life felt over in the wake of Daniel's death, she could—must—be the catalyst to bring out the potential of young girls. The males in society might want to write them off as mothers, washerwomen, skivvies, but for her, it didn't—and wouldn't—be that way.

There was a knock at her parlour door, not that you could tell it was a parlour with just the one chair in there. All the rooms were equally sparse in her new 'home.' The furniture in their tiny Hampstead flat barely filled one floor in the new Grantchester cottage, and a lot of it she couldn't bear to touch, the memories still too painful.

"Reverend Bennett, Amelia."

She smiled and waved her hand for him to come in. He was about to offer some sort of consoling, comforting words before Amelia took control of the conversation.

"Simeon, how nice to see you. How are you?"

"Er. Fine. Thank you. I've had a busy day. I've just come back from Cambridge with Thomas. And you, my dear, here on your own. How—"

She cut him off before he could finish, preferring to tread a fine line between a widow's respect and a determination to move on.

"I am keeping myself well. Ever since I arrived, I've been passing the time staring out of this window, Simeon. I find the views so peaceful. It's good for my broken spirit."

The reverend strolled over to the almost floor-to-ceiling opening and looked out, hands behind his back, rocking on his heels. The morning sunlight lit his face and his grey suit with a golden warmth.

"Yes, it is wonderful. Especially today."

"It's such a shame the children won't be able to enjoy it for some time to come. I had hoped someone would bring me some news, but not yet. Perhaps they are letting me grieve?"

The reverend's head nodded slowly then fell as a mark of respect.

"I don't suppose I could throw myself on your mercy, could I?"

"How so?"

"I know it would mean a lot to my dear Daniel, looking down on us, to see those youngsters be nurtured, cared for, to flourish. And I am sure it would bring cheer to my life too. When we reviewed the report on how to set up an orphanage, it was a lot of work for the two of us. Now there's just me, well, I am terrified my dream of helping the children will die with him. Is there any way you could convince some of the local philanthropists to rescue me, your London contacts at Tynedale perhaps?"

He said nothing. Frustration gripped Amelia, but lashing out would achieve nothing. *'Maybe he doesn't want to help just yet? Daniel's not even cold in the ground? But I have wanted this for months, and I need the help now!'*

Simeon ran his index finger along the inside of his dog collar, then clasped his hands in front of his stomach, twiddling his thumbs.

"Leave it with me," he said in a deadpan voice.

She looked at him, hoping he would elucidate.

"I'll be off then, Mrs Astley. Good day."

Amelia exhaled through her nose so quickly her nostrils hissed, and her eyelids quivered as she held them tightly shut for an eternity. *'What is the point of even trying?'*

22

THE DELIGHTFUL OFFER

The point became clear as Reverend Bennett came good on his promise. Soon work was underway on the barn, and suitable girls were being selected by Sister Nancy.

Now Amelia's life was settling, and Daniel's estate was dealt with, Thomas and Elizabeth (at Elizabeth's insistence) embarked on a Grand Tour of Europe.

"It will be fun to follow in the footsteps of the Georgian Macaronis. Swim in the crystal clear Italian waters at the Bay of Poets. I can be Byron. You can be Shelley."

"Good grief! Macaronis? Damned effeminate fellows, Elizabeth. And didn't Shelley drown there? After he was shipwrecked?"

"Why are you always such a killjoy, Thomas. We shall see Paris together, then cross the Alps. Turin, Venice for the carnival, the forum at Rome—"

"We?"

"Yes. We! And it will be wonderful." she said firmly, jabbing her curmudgeonly husband in the ribs.

Their trip also freed up Sarah and Victor, who were delighted to help Amelia set up the new facilities. Victor rolled his sleeves up and got on with the building and landscaping work. Sarah stitched a myriad of curtains, hemmed the edges of blankets, and made the place feel homely. She must have made thousands of meals and cuppas for the labourers.

"There will be many more to cook for. Think how much fun it will be if you decide to stay on to look after the pupils?" said Amelia half-jokingly, as Sarah viciously scrubbed at a baked-on pan.

Alas, Amelia's ability to muck in was limited not just because society expected her to drop into polite obscurity during the grieving process but carrying and giving birth to twins—a boy and a girl—had meant the young mother was simply better suited to paperwork and organising.

Each night, over dinner, Sarah and Victor would report back on progress and discuss Amelia's plans for the next day's tasks. Her two most-trusted companions then ensured the workmen followed the instructions to the letter the next day.

Little by little, from her parlour window, Amelia saw the building take shape. Little Thomas would sit on her lap, listening intently as she pointed out the new features, telling him how well it progressed. Then there were plenty of tall tales about the ragged little children who might eventually move there.

*

"Letter for you, for Reverend Bennett," Amelia
advised Jimmy, one of Tynedale Hall's postboys.

Dearest Simeon,

I am writing to you with good news. Thanks to your generous support of the past months, the orphanage, school, and bunks are almost complete.

The university's Head of Charitable work has written to Prince George, Duke of Cambridge, who has agreed to attend the opening ceremony and be a patron.

Having such a high-profile supporter will certainly raise our profile in philanthropic circles, and I hope and attract more donations for the orphanage. There is always more that can be done to help these poor unfortunates.

The chancellor was keen for the prince to lay the foundation stone, but I convinced him to bestow the honour on someone else. I would be most delighted if you would take on that duty. Without your help, guidance, and powerful connections, I am sure the project would have run aground by now.

RSVP

Amelia Astley
Dove Cottage Orphanage, Grantchester, Cambridge

Victor nearly took the parlour door off its hinges when he burst in to tell her Simeon had sent a telegram agreeing to her proposal.

Amelia chose May Beadle for the grand opening. Although she had only been in Granchester for a year, her life had changed immeasurably. Her plans for a new life in the country had been dashed, and her husband's life was cut short on their pretty little cottage driveway the day they arrived.

Now she stood at the freshly painted entrance to a homely, bright, and spacious orphanage, ready to accept its first intake of children, greeting royalty, with a crowd of onlookers from down the road in the village, Cambridge dons, and wealthy business owners from the City of London who had hired her beloved Daniel.

Daniel's death had been a cruel blow, but the sadness had tugged on the heartstrings of benefactors much harder, and sizable donations from Simeon's network of philanthropists had flowed in thick and fast. With Daniel's estate and her savings, plus the generosity of others, she had been able to increase capacity from the ten places she originally imagined to thirty-two, making it one of the biggest rural orphanages in the county.

"Mrs Astley, how wonderful to see you looking so well!" cheered Simeon as he approached.

"I've been looking for you," she said with a grin, handing him a silver trowel and a large grey block with an inscription.

He glanced down to read it, swallowing ever harder the more words his eyes scanned.

Dove Cottage Orphanage

Established 1 May 1896

This stone was laid by Reverend Bennett of Tynedale Hall London, who was instrumental in its foundation.

"May the Lord reward you for your kindness."

Victor held out a small board with some mortar.

"Would you like me to set it for you, reverend?"

"No, no. You can teach me what to do. This is a place of learning after all," he added cheerfully. "Just make sure I don't get mortar all over me, Victor. I have spent my life working in buildings, not on them."

Amelia chuckled as she watched Simeon try to spread the cement evenly on the stone and keep it stuck on as he offered it up to the hole in the wall. He was all fingers and thumbs. Victor had to try awfully hard not to take over.

"The children should be here any minute with Sister Nancy. They are processing up from the church."

It was Amelia's turn to well up as she saw a troop of little city children snaking their way up the lane towards their new home, their heads spinning around, taking in all the new sights, sounds and smells. The teachers met the children by the gate and offered them finger sandwiches and fresh lemonade. They didn't know what to make of it. It was then she wondered what Daniel would have said to them on their arrival. He was wonderful at putting people at ease. The thought stung, and she wanted to banish it and yet treasure it at the same time. Taking Simeon and Sister Nancy on a tour of the buildings spared her from openly crying in front of everyone.

> "Here on the ground floor is the boy's dormitory. Space for sixteen of them. There's a wood-burning fire at each end to keep them warm in the winter, and Sarah has done a wonderful job with the thick curtains. They will make it wonderfully dark here in the summer."

Sister Nancy ran her hand over the plush fabric and smiled. It was a lot better than the old ship's sails that had been adapted for the mission. Simeon gave the bunk bed mattresses a prod and felt the quality of them instantly.

> "Upstairs, the girl's facilities are laid out the same. And this little annexe room is where the dormitory master sleeps, so we can keep an eye on them. I know what I was like at their age."

Sister Nancy gave a knowing look.

> "Across the yard are the classrooms, shall we?"

The yard was spotless, nothing like the muddy wasteland it had been when Amelia moved in. On the floor, Victor had painted hopscotch grids for the girls, and on the solid walls at either end, the lines to make up simple goalposts for the lads to play football.

"Unlike other schools, we chose to have our windows lower so the children could see out onto the rolling hills. It helps illuminate the desks. And thanks to the extra money, we have been able to add solid walls between the classrooms, rather than rely on screens or curtains. Each room has a map of the world and a blackboard. The younger children use chalk and slates, but we are encouraging the older ones to use ink pens."

The new blackboard had its first lesson chalked upon it.

2 farthings = 1 halfpenny

2 halfpence = 1 penny

6 pence = 1 sixpence (a 'tanner') (6d)

12 pence = 1 shilling (a bob) (1s)

"And for those children who are less academically minded, we have an outbuilding where they can learn practical skills like ironmongery and basket weaving. Local business owners and

manufacturers have donated some of their old
equipment for us, and the older children will get
apprenticeships."

"Well, I must say, it's an amazing place, Mrs
Astley," said Sister Nancy, giving Amelia the first
piece of praise she could remember from her in
years.

"Sister Nancy and I will continue to support you.
Please keep us informed. And if you need
anything, please let us know."

Eventually, the crowd made its way back to Grantchester
then onto their homes.

Amelia, Sarah, and Victor checked the children were fed
and settled, then made sure the new teachers were happy
in their quarters. It had been a punishingly long day for
everyone. The trio of friends returned to Dove Cottage,
exhausted but delighted with how the grand opening had
gone.

"I don't know about you, but I need a sherry," said
Amelia, rubbing her aching back as she reached
for the decanter.

"Good idea," the other two replied.

Sarah flopped in the rocking chair in the parlour and took
off her smart new work boots. She regretted not wearing
them more before, as she spotted angry blisters on her little toes. Victor slumped in the corner of the new chaise
longue.

"A toast to our hard work is in order, I think," said Amelia, standing looking out towards the valley, then back into the room.

Then upstairs there was: *'waah.'* The twins had woken wanting something. The three of them looked at each other, glasses in hand, wondering whose turn it was.

"I'll go," said Sarah, grunting as she got to her feet.

Victor looked at Amelia, amazed at how well she had coped from the bitter tragedy of her arrival, in fact, all of the challenges she had faced since he met her: the icy dunking in the River Cherwell, nearly drowning in the boat she made with Thomas, the cruel treatment she had received from the likes of Gerald, and all the work to set up the orphanage whilst expecting twins. She was a miracle, and he was determined not to lose her heart to something or someone else again.

"Do you remember the night at Thomas and Elizabeth's wedding reception at Randolph?"

"Yes, it was quite a night. Do you remember his dancing? I could barely breathe from laughing."

"Well, you were supposed to meet me. I was going to speak to you about something?"

"You've got a good memory! Yes, I think you were."

The nervous young man fumbled in his pocket for the little box he had kept since that night.

"I bet you can remember what you were going to say too?"

"Yes, very well, Amelia. Like it was yesterday," he said, knocking back his sherry in one, then pretending to need another glass.

But he didn't walk to the decanter. He walked to her. She looked puzzled, then everything became clear.

"Amelia, will you marry me?"

Yet again, she fought back the tears that day as she hugged him with all her might. She buried her face in the comforting nape of his neck.

"Yes! Of course, I will," came the muffled reply.

***

Other books in The Whitechapel Girls series:

The Workhouse Waif's Remedy

The Whitechapel slums are unforgiving, and for young Mabel, the loss of both parents means she must now fight alone.

Rejected by everyone in her tenement, only the doors of the workhouse will open.

Determined to survive the ordeal, her only hope is to align herself with powerful characters, those who might offer a faint glimmer of hope and kindness within the hellish institution.

But not everyone thinks the hardworking inmate deserves a lucky break and the powers that be are keen to smash her dreams and keep her trapped.

Will she crumble and let the bullies steal the joy and love from her life? Or does she have one final trick up her sleeve to thrive?

A heartwarming and touching Victorian romance. Join Mabel in her emotional fight for love, independence and a brighter future.

Click to buy the Workhouse Waif's Remedy now.

AUTHOR'S NOTE

My inspiration for Amelia.

Sabrina Bicknell (1757 – 8 September 1843), also known as Sabrina Sidney, was a British lady who was abandoned as a newborn at the Foundling Hospital in London and adopted at the age of 12 by the eccentric novelist and philosopher Thomas Day, who sought to mould her into his ideal bride. Instead, she grew up to marry one of Day's friends and ultimately became a school manager.

After being rejected by multiple women and unable to find a partner who shared his ideas, Day chose to teach two daughters, using his own notions, inspired by Jean-Jacques Rousseau's work 'Emile, or On Education'. In 1769, Day and his lawyer buddy, John Bicknell, selected Sidney and another girl, Lucretia, from orphanages and falsely announced that they would be indentured to Day's acquaintance Richard Lovell Edgeworth. Day travelled with the girls to France to implement Rousseau's techniques of teaching in isolation. He returned to Lichfield with just Sidney after deciding that Lucretia was unsuitable for his experiment. To improve her fortitude, he utilised strange, quirky, and often harsh procedures like shooting blanks at her skirts, putting hot wax on her arms, and having her walk into a lake fully clad to test her resistance to cold water.

Sidney was born in Clerkenwell, London, in 1757 and was abandoned by an unidentified person on May 24, 1757, at the Hospital for the Maintenance and Education of Exposed and Deserted Young Children (more generally known as the Foundling Hospital). The individual left a letter stating that the baby's baptismal name was Manima Butler, and was baptised at St James's Church in Clerkenwell. Her name was most likely a typo of Monimia, but the church has no baptismal records for any form of the name.

Thomas Day was a bachelor who had inherited his father's riches as a baby. Day studied philosophy at Corpus Christi College in Oxford, where he was described as having a smallpox-pockmarked face, a gloomy attitude, and a sharp temper. It was then that he resolved to devote his life to become a moral man, eschewing luxury in favour of selflessness. Around the same time, he made a list of prerequisites for his future wife, including the need for her to be submissive and pure while still being able to talk philosophy and live without frivolities. Because of his high standards and his generally dislikeable nature, numerous women turned down his approaches while he was in university.

Day was exposed to Jean-Jacques Rousseau's writings by his friend Richard Lovell Edgeworth; the two had a special fondness for Rousseau's work on education in 'Emile, or On Education.'

On leaving Oxford, Edgeworth and Day attempted to teach Edgeworth's first son in the style of Emile, a learning-by-doing approach.

While accompanying Edgeworth to Ireland as the boy's teacher, Day fell in love and was rejected by both Edgeworth's sister and at least three other ladies in rapid succession.

Day concluded that he would be unable to find a bride who met his high standards, partly due to his thoughts on women's education. Inspired by Sophie in Rousseau's Emile, he planned to 'make' his perfect bride by nurturing her from childhood. Day was nearing financial independence and plotted with his barrister friend, John Bicknell, to bring two females to his home.

In June 1769, just after Day's 21st birthday, he and John Bicknell travelled to the Shrewsbury Orphan Hospital to choose the first female for their experiment. Sidney was 12 at the time, and she was characterised as "a clear auburn brunette, with deeper eyes more brilliant bloom and chestnut hair." She was slim, with long lashes and a nice voice. Day was having trouble deciding on a female for the experiment when Bicknell stepped in. The experiment was kept a secret from the orphanage secretary, Samuel Magee. Instead, they informed him that she would be indentured as a servant at Edgeworth's country estate in Berkshire. Edgeworth would be legally responsible for Sidney, despite the fact that he was not present or even aware of the arrangement, following the orphanage's requirement that responsibility be held by a respectable married man.

The orphanage directors accepted the apprenticeship on June 30, 1769, and Day and Bicknell collected Sidney on August 17, 1769.

Day's name was changed to Sabrina Sidney: Sabrina is the Latin name for the River Severn, which her orphanage overlooked, and Sidney is named after Algernon Sidney, one of Day's idols. Day later became a donor and administrator of the Foundling Hospital, and on September 20, 1769, he picked another child for his experiment, dubbing her Lucretia after the Roman matron.

Day asked Bicknell to draught a document outlining the conditions of the girls' indenture. He would pick which girl he wanted to marry within a year, and the other would be handed as an apprentice to a lady in a trade for a cost of £100. He would add another £400 if the girl married or started her own company. He would marry his chosen wife or, if he did not, he would give her £500. Bicknell served as the contract's guarantor.

Day wanted the girls to be separated from other influences while he schooled them, so he planned to relocate them to France in early November 1769. It's also plausible that he did this to shield himself from the legal consequences of his experiment, as well as social gossip. The three drove almost 370 miles to Avignon, where they rented a property. The girls couldn't speak French, and Day didn't hire any English-speaking employees to ensure that he was the only one who could influence them.

In the Emile tradition, the day was centred on the education of the females. He supplemented the Foundling

Hospital's instruction in reading and basic mathematics and taught them how to write. He thought that the girls should be competent to run the home. Thus they were assigned tasks such as cooking, cleaning, and other housekeeping. Finally, he wanted them to be able to argue complicated ideas with them, so he taught them basic physics and geography theories, assigning them the duty of watching the change of the seasons and noting details of sunrises and sunsets. He also instilled in them Rousseau's intellectual disdain for luxury.

During his time in France, Day kept in touch with Edgeworth regularly. He said that both girls were enthusiastic about their academics, with Sidney being the more so. Day also shared experiences, including one about a vacation on the Rhone when the boat capsized, and he had to rescue both females by himself since neither could swim. He mentioned an occasion in which he challenged a French Army officer to a duel, even presenting a pair of duelling pistols, only to engage or encourage discourse with his young pupils; the officer apologised and said he meant no offence, calming the situation.

According to accounts by 19th-century historians, Day got frustrated with the girls when they were bored with their studies and started to bicker, and he also spent a large amount of time nursing them through an episode of smallpox.

While in France, Day was debating which female to choose to carry out the experiment. Lucretia was more joyful, whereas Sidney was more quiet and studious.

When the three returned to England in the spring of 1770, Day had finally chosen to continue Sidney's schooling. Edgeworth added that although each of Day's initiatives with Sabrina had been successful, he had concluded that Lucretia was 'invincibly dumb.' Day apprenticed Lucretia to a milliner on Ludgate Hill and brought Sidney to Stowe House in Lichfield to complete her education. The residence would have had just a few servants, leaving Sidney to manage the household. Her tuition continued at the same time, with Day giving her one-on-one sessions on a range of topics.

Day continued to instruct Sidney to strengthen her against adversity, based on his reading of Rousseau's Emile. The book discusses the notion of 'negative education,' which involves shielding a person from vices rather than teaching them virtues. Day understood this to suggest that subjecting Sidney to endurance tests would aid in developing a lady with hardened nerves. Rousseau used the example of assisting Emile to grow acclimated to explosions such as fireworks by shooting handguns with little quantities of powder near him and progressively increasing the quantity of powder. On the other hand, Day fired a loaded handgun at Sidney's petticoat without informing her there was no shot in it.

He would put hot sealing wax on her back and arms or stick pins in her, telling her not to scream out in an effort to improve her pain tolerance. He would put her capacity to keep secrets to the test by telling her that his life was in danger and that she should not inform anybody. Day advised Sidney to wade into Stowe Pool until the water reached her neck, then sleep in the neighbouring meadow until her clothing and hair had dried in the sun. Finally, to put her to the test, he brought her a large package of hand-crafted silk clothing and told her to burn them. Day's effectiveness with these tactics was limited. Sidney learned not to flinch when hot wax was spilt on her arm, but she did warn others about his secret tactics and could-n't stop screaming whenever he fired his pistol at her.

During their stay at Stowe House, Day introduced Sidney to members of the local intellectual society, notably Thomas Seward, the priest at Lichfield Cathedral. Seward and his wife felt that Day would be a suitable suitor for their daughter, Anna, and her letters reveal her interest in Day. Sidney, who became the conduit between Day and the Seward family, captivated Anna as well

By 1770, Sidney was questioning Day's methods and com-plaining about the duties given to her.

The appropriateness of Day's relationship with Sidney was called into question by the local community. Edge-worth joined Day for Christmas at Stowe and persuaded him that his experiment had failed. He also convinced Day that Sidney was too old to live with him without supervi-sion. Day seemed to agree with Edgeworth's assessment. He paid for Sidney to attend Sutton Coldfield boarding school in Warwickshire in early 1771. She spent three years in the boarding school, including weekends and hol-idays, with sporadic visits from Day. Normally, the school concentrated on preparing high-society girls for mar-riage, including embroidery and the arts. Day specified that she should be taught academic courses but not dance or learn music.

In 1774, Day paid a visit to Sidney to tell her she would be apprenticed to the Parkinsons, a dressmaking family, since Day felt the occupation would keep her from temptation. She was given to the family on the condition that she worked hard at housework and was denied any luxury. The Parkinsons, on the other hand, treated Sidney so nicely that Day later reprimanded them for not instilling 'industry and frugality' in her.

Less than a year later, the Parkinsons' company failed, leaving Sidney without an apprenticeship and no place to live. Day arranged for her to stay with his friends, the Keir family, and suggested that she work as a housekeeper in his own home. Day considered Sidney, who was now eighteen, as a prospective wife again but did not inform her of his plans or that her upbringing was part of his experiment.

Over the following six months, Day returned to shaping Sidney into the perfect lady, deciding what she would wear and imposing his views of thrift on her. Day assumed he had finally developed a lady who would fit all of his needs when Sidney enthusiastically accepted all of the suggestions. He was so sure of himself that he freely discussed marrying Sidney, despite the fact that she was oblivious of his plans. One of Day's friends eventually told her that he wished to marry her. Sidney questioned Day about the rumours, and he confirmed they were genuine, omitting to explain that he had intended to marry her from the first time they met.

Sidney did not reject the proposal, so Day arranged the wedding while she deliberated and finally consented.

Day left Sabrina with friends for a few days during the preparations, giving her explicit instructions on what to wear. When he returned to discover her dressed inappropriately, he erupted into a frenzy. Sabrina disappeared for a few hours, so Day called off the engagement. She was sent to a Birmingham boarding house and granted a stipend of £50 per year. Day vowed to never see her again.

Sidney spent eight years in boarding homes throughout Birmingham after her engagement to Thomas ended. In 1778, Day met and married an heiress, Esther Milnes.

Sabrina had become a lady's companion in Newport, Shropshire, in 1783. John Bicknell, Day's friend and the fellow who helped choose her at the foundling hospital, contacted her there. Bicknell was a single man who had spent the bulk of his legal earnings on gaming establishments. He hadn't paid much attention to Sidney since Day chose her, but he proposed marriage right away.

Sidney discussed the proposed engagement with Day once again. Day did not approve, arguing that the age gap was too wide, even though Bicknell was just two years older than Day. Bicknell decided to tell the girl the truth about the experiment, that she had been hand-picked to be Day's wife from infancy, and that all of Day's actions were planned to help him achieve his objective of making her the perfect bride. Sidney was terrified and wrote to Day to confront him about Bicknell's accusations. Day acknowledged the facts but refused to apologise. After a series of letters, Thomas consented to the marriage, assuring her that the letter would be his last connection with her.

Bicknell and Sidney married on April 16, 1784, in Birmingham's St Philip's Cathedral. On the same day, Day paid the £500 wedding dowry mandated in his contract with Bicknell, thereby terminating his £50 a year stipend.

The couple settled in Shenfield and had two sons, John Laurens Bicknell and Henry Edgeworth Bicknell. Bicknell continued to gamble, wasting the family's remaining funds over the next three years. After three years of marriage, John Bicknell died of a paralytic stroke on March 27, 1787.

Sabrina and her two children were suddenly without a source of income. Day handed her a new stipend of £30 per year, which Edgeworth matched. Friends of her husband's barristers contributed £8000 for the widow and her children. Sidney worked as a housekeeper for Charles Burney and as the general manager of his schools in London. Her own children were taught at his Greenwich school.

After Day's death in 1789, his widow, Esther, continued to pay Sidney's stipend, and Sabrina worked with Burney until she was 68. She was residing in a four-storey mansion in Gloucester Circus, Greenwich, with her own maids.

Sabrina Sidney died at home on September 8, 1843, due to a severe asthma attack. She was laid to rest at Kensal Green Cemetery.

ABOUT THE AUTHOR

I live with my cat, Ralph, in Somerset. I love finding real stories and turning them into romance sagas. There are so many fascinating people and places to weave into an interesting tale. It's a real privilege to write them.

You can follow me on my Amazon author page or find out more on my website. I love to hear from my readers.

Thank you for all your support.

Beryl

www.berylwhite.co.uk